Meringues and Murder

A Cozy Mystery in Venice (Whispering Pines Cozy Mysteries Book 5)

Penelope Loveletter

LOVELETTER
PUBLICATIONS
EST. 2023

LOVELETTER PUBLICATIONS

Other Books in the Whispering Pines Series

All books in the Whispering Pines Series may be read as Stand-Alones

<u>Whispering Pines Sweet Romances:</u>

Whispers by the Lake

Whispers of the Heart

Whispers of Forever

<u>Whispering Pines Cozy Mysteries:</u>

Whispers of Murder (Whispering Pines Cozy Mystery Book 1)

Whispers of Death (Whispering Pines Cozy Mystery Book 2)

Whispers of Mystery (Whispering Pines Cozy Mystery Book 3)

<u>Whispers in Europe Cozy Mysteries:</u>

Macarons and Murder- A Cozy Mystery in Paris
(Whispering Pines Cozy Mystery Book 4)

Meringues and Murder- A Cozy Mystery in Venice
(Whispering Pines Cozy Mystery Book 5)

Dedication

Dedicated to Alan

Thank you for turning Venice from a nightmare to a dream come true.

Contents

Meringues
and
Murder

Chapter 1

E mma Harper stepped off the bus. She pulled her long red hair to the side and her eyes widened as she took in the scene before her. Venice!

Sunlight danced on the emerald waters of the Grand Canal, casting a golden glow on the weathered facades of centuries-old buildings. Boats bobbed along the edge of the canal waiting to take visitors to the many sights.

She took in a deep breath and closed her eyes as she felt the glow of the afternoon sun on her face. "Daniel, pinch me. I can't believe we're actually here," she said, squeezing his hand.

He smiled, pulling her close, his blue eyes matching the summer blue sky. "No pinching necessary. But how about a kiss?"

She tipped her face to his, but as she did so, her stomach twisted in discomfort.

"Oh," she groaned. "Still not feeling great."

Daniel gave her a quick kiss on her cheek before he grabbed their suitcases. "That's no fun," he said as she looped her hand through the crook of his elbow. They wove through the throng of tourists and locals, the streets echoing with different languages. A group of pigeons took flight as they passed, startling Emma.

"Look at that!" She pointed to a nearby bridge, its graceful arch spanning the narrow waterway. "Is that the Rialto?"

Daniel shook his head. "I don't think so. There are hundreds of bridges in Venice. But I think we'll see the Rialto tomorrow, when we tour the city."

"I hope I'll feel better by then," Emma said shaking her head. It was wonderful to be on her dream vacation with her boyfriend, Daniel. But it was torture to be sick and unable to really enjoy it.

This vacation had been years in the planning, and for several months before they left their hometown of Whispering Pines, Minnesota, it had looked like they wouldn't be able to go at all. Daniel's department at the police station where he was a detective had come due for an inspection just as Emma had become tangled up in a murder mystery involving her bakery.

But they had done it! They had somehow managed to slip away for the entire summer! After several glorious weeks in Paris and southern France, they were finally in Venice- a city Emma had only ever dreamed of seeing. And if Paris hadn't been exactly the vacation she'd been hoping for- given the murder to solve- Emma hoped that would all be behind them now and they could simply enjoy their time in Venice.

This was assuming whatever bug she'd caught would let her.

As they walked along one of the smaller canals, a gondolier called out to them. "*Signore e signora!* Gondola ride?"

Emma shook her head. "Not today, thank you."

The gondolier tipped his hat and smiled as they continued across a small bridge and along a narrow pedestrian-only street which Emma gathered, from the tiles with street names set into the buildings along the way, must be called *calles* in Italian.

Emma had her phone out, navigating toward their hotel as they walked, and her gaze darted from centuries-old buildings to the colorful flower boxes hanging from wrought-iron balconies.

"Oh, Daniel, look!" Emma exclaimed, pointing to a small bridge ahead. "I think that's the Bridge of Sighs."

As they approached, Emma admired the stone carvings on the passageway. "Can you imagine being a prisoner here in the Middle Ages? Seeing Venice for the last time through those tiny windows?"

Daniel shook his head. "It's hard to believe something so beautiful has such a morbid history."

They paused on the bridge, watching another gondola pass beneath them. The passengers, a young couple, were holding hands and smiled up at them.

Emma smiled and nudged Daniel with her shoulder. "I guess some things are universal, no matter where you are."

Her heart raced with excitement as she and Daniel approached the grand expanse of Piazza San Marco. The imposing facade of St. Mark's Basilica loomed before them, its Byzantine domes and intricate mosaics glittering in the late afternoon sun.

"It's even more beautiful than the pictures," Emma whispered, her eyes wide as she took in the ornate details of the cathedral's exterior.

Daniel nodded, his arm wrapped around her waist. "I can't wait to see the inside."

As they drew closer, Emma marveled at the elaborate golden mosaics on the arches above the entrance. The winged lion of St. Mark, symbol of Venice, gazed down at them from its perch on top of one of the cathedral's pillars.

A flock of pigeons scattered as they crossed the square, their wings fluttering against the backdrop of the basilica's marble columns. Emma inhaled deeply, savoring the mix of sea air and the faint scent of espresso.

"Look at those horses," Daniel pointed to the replicas of the famous bronze horses atop the *loggia*. "I think I read that the originals are inside the museum and were made in Greece around the 4th century BC."

Emma's gaze followed his gesture, then swept across the bustling piazza. Street vendors hawked their wares, tourists snapped photos, and the melodic strains of a violinist drifted through the air.

"And to think that back home, my bakery is considered old because it was built in 1915!"

They both laughed. As they circled the cathedral, Emma looked down at the intricate patterns of the marble floor beneath their feet. She paused, tracing a swirling design with the toe of her shoe.

"It's like walking through ancient history," she murmured.

Daniel squeezed her hand. "Speaking of history, want to check out the Doge's Palace next door?"

Emma nodded, but as they turned toward the palace, a wave of nausea washed over her. She gripped Daniel's arm for support.

"Em? You okay?"

She took a deep breath and forced a smile. "I'm sorry. Maybe we can do the Doge's Palace another day?"

They crossed the piazza and continued into a narrow side street- although the word street, Emma thought, implied cars. And there were certainly no cars here. The *calle* walkways were clearly built centuries before anyone dreamed of an automobile.

"Look at that!" She pointed to a nearby bridge where a street musician played his violin.

The scent of freshly baked bread and espresso wafted from a nearby café, and Emma's stomach growled, reminding her of her uneaten meal on the plane.

"We should grab a bite to eat soon," Daniel suggested, noticing her discomfort. "Maybe some authentic Italian pizza?"

Emma shook her head as another wave of nausea washed over her. "I'm really not feeling great."

Daniel's brow furrowed. "Could it be from that fish you had last night? You said it smelled a little off."

Emma sighed, remembering how she'd ignored her instincts and eaten the questionable meal anyway. "You're probably right. I don't know why I never trust myself. I figured it had to be fine. Your meal was great, right?"

Daniel nodded and Emma sighed.

"So I thought I must be imagining it." She put her hand back on her stomach and looked away as they passed a sidewalk cafe with aromatic pizzas. "Ok, definitely shouldn't have eaten the fish. I can't believe I'm in Italy and don't want to eat pizza!"

As they continued, Emma's excitement dampened by her growing queasiness. The charm of Venice's winding alleys and picturesque canals was still evident, but she found herself longing for nothing more than a comfortable bed and a glass of ginger ale.

She leaned against Daniel as they crossed another arched bridge, its weathered stone cool beneath her palm. The canal below shimmered in the early evening sunlight, a gondola gliding silently past.

"Look at how the gondolier stands," Emma said. "It's like he's part of the boat."

Daniel nodded, his arm tightening around her waist. "I've heard it takes years of practice to master that skill."

As they reached the other side of the bridge, a melodic voice drifted up from the water. The gondolier, wearing the traditional striped shirt and straw hat, was serenading his passengers with an Italian love song.

Emma closed her eyes and smiled. "I never thought I'd hear a real gondolier sing. This is magical. Even if I feel like I'm going to barf." She gave a sad snort that was half laughter, half desire to get something for her stomach.

They continued down a narrow street, their shoulders brushing the ancient brick walls. Wrought-iron lamps flickered on, casting a warm glow over the cobblestones, and the scent of jasmine wafted from a nearby window box.

The streets widened, opening into a bustling square lined with outdoor cafés. The sound of laughter, clinking glasses, and music filled the air as locals and tourists alike enjoyed *aperitivo*, an Italian pre-meal that involves drinking and eating before dinner to stimulate the appetite.

Daniel grinned. "Feeling up to it? Want to join the locals for a drink?"

Emma's stomach lurched at the thought. "Maybe tomorrow. I think I need to lie down for a bit."

Finally, as they rounded a corner, Emma looked up from the map on her phone and her face lit up. "There it is! Pasticceria Ricci."

The tiny bakery was visible along the narrow *calle*, its faded frescoes and bougainvillea-framed doorway exactly matching the photos they'd seen online. Emma managed a smile, mustering enthusiasm despite her discomfort.

"It's lovely," she said. "It's so cute that I was half expecting to find out they'd made up those photos online. But it's actually even more adorable in real life." She smiled at him.

Daniel pushed open the door, and several small bells tinkled overhead. The interior was a feast for the senses, with antique wooden shelves lined with colorful nougats, pastel meringues, and delicate pastries. Behind the worn marble counter stood a robust woman with salt-and-pepper curls tied back in a loose ponytail.

"*Benvenuti!*" the woman called out cheerfully. "Welcome to Pasticceria Ricci. How can I help you?"

Daniel stepped forward and dropped the suitcases he'd been carrying, his eyes roving over the display cases. "Everything looks amazing. I'll have a cannoli and an espresso, please."

Emma hung back, her stomach churning at the thought of food.

"And for you, *cara*?" The woman tipped her head as she looked Emma up and down. "You look a little pale. Perhaps some chamomile tea?"

Emma nodded. "That would be perfect, thank you."

"My name is Lucia. Anything I can get for you, you let me know."

As Lucia busied herself with their order,

Daniel said, "Thank you, Lucia. I'm Daniel Lindberg, by the way, and this is Emma Harper."

Lucia's eyes lit up with recognition, her face breaking into a wide grin. "Ah! The American couple! I've been waiting for you all day!" She bustled around the counter wiping her flour-dusted hands on her colorful apron. "Welcome, welcome! I'm so pleased you're finally here. And you'll be here for two weeks! That's wonderful!"

Emma couldn't help but smile at Lucia's enthusiasm, despite her lingering nausea. The older woman's joy was infectious.

"We're so excited to be here," Emma managed. "Your bakery is even more beautiful than the pictures."

Lucia beamed at the compliment. "*Grazie, cara*. But you look tired from your journey. Let me show you to your room so you can rest."

She turned to Daniel. "And you, young man, can help me with the luggage."

As they followed Lucia up a narrow staircase to the second floor, Emma felt relief wash over her. The thought of a comfortable bed and a quiet room was incredibly appealing.

Lucia chattered away as they climbed, her voice filled with warmth and excitement. "Two weeks! We'll have so much time together. And you are a baker, yes? I'll teach you all about Venetian pastries, Emma. And Daniel, I know all the best spots in the city for a romantic evening."

Emma glanced at Daniel, seeing her own mix of amusement and gratitude reflected in his eyes. They'd barely arrived, and already Lucia was treating them like family.

Lucia chatted about the bakery's history and the rooms they'd be staying in. Emma tried to focus on the conversation, but her discomfort was making it difficult to concentrate.

Finally, Lucia unlocked an ancient wooden door, revealing a cozy space with a twin bed, a small balcony overlooking a quiet canal, and a vase of small blue flowers beside the window.

"It's beautiful," Emma murmured, taking in the view of weathered buildings and a gondola gliding by.

Lucia beamed with pride. "Rest up, and when you're feeling better, I'll give you my favorite recommendations for dinner. There are so many places right here," she motioned out the window, "on this very street. And Daniel, your room is just across the hall." She showed him his door.

Emma smiled to herself, thinking the word "hall" was generous for the tiny space between her room and Daniel's.

Daniel dropped his bag in his room and returned to Emma's.

As the door closed behind Lucia, Emma sank onto the bed with a groan. "I'm so sorry, Daniel. I know you wanted to explore the city today."

Daniel sat beside her, rubbing her back gently. "Hey, don't worry about it. We have plenty of time. Why don't you get some rest? I'll go pick up some medicine and see if I can find ginger ale for you. Or maybe they'll have ginger tea in the pharmacy."

Emma nodded, grateful for his understanding. As Daniel headed out, she curled up on the bed, listening to the distant sounds of Venice through the open window. Despite her illness, a smile tugged at her lips. They were in Venice, and soon enough, she'd be better, and able to embrace every moment of their romantic getaway.

Chapter 2

Emma awoke to the sound of church bells and the gentle lapping of water against the canal outside. She stretched, pleasantly surprised to find her nausea had subsided and wondered what had woken her.

Tap. Tap. It was Daniel tapping on her door.

"How are you feeling?" he asked, poking his head inside the room after she said, "Come in!"

"Much better," Emma said as she sat up in bed. "I think I might even be up for some breakfast."

They made their way downstairs to find Lucia already bustling about the bakery. The aroma of fresh bread and coffee filled the air.

"Ah, good morning!" Lucia called out. "You look much improved, Emma. Hungry?"

Emma nodded. "Starving, actually. Everything smells amazing."

As they settled at a small table, Daniel said, "We were hoping you might recommend a gondolier. We'd love to see Venice from the water."

Lucia's face lit up. "Oh, I know just the person! Valentina Rossi. She's one of the few female gondoliers in Venice. Smart as a whip and knows the city like the back of her hand."

"A female gondolier?" Emma perked up. "That's fantastic."

Lucia nodded. "She had to fight hard for her place. Let me give her a call."

As Lucia dialed, Emma and Daniel exchanged excited glances. Lucia's rapid-fire Italian filled the bakery as she chatted with Valentina.

"Perfect!" Lucia hung up the phone. "Valentina will meet you at the *Ponte dei Sospiri* dock in an hour. It's not far, I can draw you a map."

"Thank you so much, Lucia," Emma said. "We really appreciate your help."

Lucia waved her hand dismissively. "Nonsense. Now, eat up! You'll need your strength for all the sightseeing."

As they finished their breakfast, Emma felt a surge of excitement. She was finally feeling well enough to truly experience Venice, and she couldn't wait to meet Valentina and see the city from a female gondolier's unique perspective.

Emma and Daniel strolled hand in hand along the cobblestone streets, following Lucia's hand-drawn map. As the Ponte dei Sospiri dock came into view, Emma spotted two figures, a man and a woman in traditional gondolier black and white striped shirts, standing near two sleek black gondolas.

"That must be her," Emma said.

As they approached, the young woman with olive skin and dark hair tied back in a neat bun waved at them. "Emma and Daniel?" she called out.

Emma nodded, smiling. "That's us. You must be Valentina."

"Welcome to Venice," Valentina said, her hazel eyes sparkling. She gestured to the man beside her. "This is my friend Giuseppe."

Giuseppe tipped his straw hat. "*Ciao*! Lovely to meet you both."

Emma couldn't help but notice how handsome Giuseppe was, with his tousled hair and charming smile. She glanced at Daniel, who was admiring the gondolas.

"Your boats are beautiful," Daniel said, and Giuseppe smiled. "Thank you! I inherited mine from my father, who inherited it from his father." He winked at Valentina. "Someday soon you will own yours as well."

Valentina raised an eyebrow as if she wasn't so sure.

"Three generations!" Daniel said. "That's impressive!"

"So, where are you from?" Giuseppe asked Emma.

"Minnesota," Emma replied. "It's quite different from Venice."

Giuseppe laughed. "I imagine so! No canals, eh?"

"Lots of lakes, and plenty of snow, but no canals," Emma agreed with a laugh.

Emma watched as Giuseppe's eyes lit up with curiosity. He leaned against the pole on the dock, his posture relaxed and inviting.

"Minnesota, eh? Tell me more about these lakes of yours," Giuseppe said, his accent adding a musical lilt to his words.

Emma smiled. "They're beautiful. We have thousands of them. In the summer, they're perfect for swimming and boating. In the winter, they freeze over and we go ice fishing and skating."

Giuseppe's eyebrows shot up. "Frozen lakes?" He laughed. "That's hard to imagine in Venice!"

"It's quite different," Emma agreed. "But I have to admit, these canals are truly magical. There's nothing like them back home."

Giuseppe nodded, then turned to Daniel. "What about you, my friend? Do you spend much time on these lakes? Fishing or rowing, perhaps?"

Daniel shook his head, a hint of regret in his voice. "Not nearly as much as I'd like. Work keeps me pretty busy most of the time."

"Ah, the curse of the modern world," Giuseppe said with a dramatic sigh. "What is it you do that keeps you from enjoying your beautiful lakes?"

"I'm a detective," Daniel replied.

Giuseppe's eyes widened with interest. "A detective? Like in the movies?"

Daniel chuckled. "Not quite as exciting, I'm afraid. Mostly paperwork and interviews. Whispering Pines isn't exactly a hotbed of crime."

"Whispering Pines?" Giuseppe repeated, testing the name on his tongue. "It sounds peaceful."

"It is," Emma chimed in, and then paused before she said, "Well, most of the time, anyway."

Giuseppe looked between them, a mischievous glint in his eye. "And yet you have a detective. Perhaps there are more secrets in Whispering Pines than meet the eye, no?" Giuseppe's grin spread from ear to ear. "Have you solved any murders?"

Daniel chuckled, running a hand through his hair. "A few, actually."

"You really have?" Valentina asked. "That's incredible!"

"Well, if you want to talk about solving murders," Daniel said, wrapping an arm around Emma's waist, "you should ask this one. She's cracked more cases than I have."

Emma felt her cheeks flush. "Daniel, please—"

"Is this true?" Giuseppe asked, his gaze darting between Emma and Daniel. "Are you both detectives?"

"No, no," Emma said, waving her hands. "I'm just a baker. Daniel's the real detective."

"A baker who solves murders?" Valentina said. "That's a story I'd love to hear."

Emma laughed. "It's not as exciting as it sounds. I just... notice things sometimes."

"She's being modest," Daniel interjected. "Emma's solved three murders back home. She's got a knack for unraveling mysteries."

Giuseppe's expression turned thoughtful. "Three murders. A baker detective... That's quite unusual. Like Valentina. You are not the typical woman."

"I'm not a detective," Emma insisted. "I just help out where I can. Sometimes that means baking, sometimes it means... well, noticing things others might miss."

"Like following crumbs at a crime scene?" Giuseppe joked, earning a laugh from the group.

"She can piece together the ingredients of a mystery," Daniel said, squeezing Emma's shoulder. "That's for certain."

Emma rolled her eyes but couldn't help smiling. "Can we please talk about something else? We're on vacation. No mysteries, no murders, just gondolas and good food."

She noticed Giuseppe looking thoughtful again, almost as if he was studying her.

"Speaking of which," Valentina said, gesturing to the gondolas, "shall we begin our tour? I promise not to steer us into any crime scenes.

Where would you two like to go today?"

Daniel looked at Emma, his eyebrows raised in question. Emma shrugged and said, "We want to see everything, really. It's our first time in Venice."

Valentina nodded, her eyes lighting up. "Of course, you are first timers! Well, there's certainly plenty to see. Any particular interests? Art, history, architecture?"

"All of the above," Emma replied, feeling a flutter of excitement despite the lingering fatigue from yesterday's bout of food poisoning. "We'd love to get a good overview of the city."

Daniel chimed in, "And maybe some insider tips on the best places to eat?"

Valentina laughed. "Of course! I know all the hidden gems. How about we do a full afternoon tour? We can cover the Grand Canal, see some of the major landmarks, and I can point out my favorite spots along the way.

"Perhaps you can end your day in the market at the Rialto Bridge," Giuseppe said. "You can do some shopping. It's amazing. You really must see it."

Again, Emma noticed his intense gaze. Was he trying to tell her something with that stare? Or just studying her? "That would be great," she said as she turned away. Perhaps he always looked at people like that.

Emma leaned into Daniel's side as they discussed the details, and he wrapped an arm around her waist.

"You okay?" he whispered.

"Just a little tired still," Emma murmured back.

Valentina added, "We can take it easy then, take extra time just enjoying the view in the gondola if you need to rest. How does that sound?"

Emma nodded gratefully. "That would be perfect, thank you."

They agreed on a price for the tour, and Valentina gestured towards her gondola. "Shall we?"

As Emma stepped into the boat, she felt it sway under her feet. She settled onto the cushioned seat, determined to enjoy every moment of their Venetian adventure, even if she had to take it a bit slower than planned.

Before she got into the gondola, Valentina tugged on Giuseppe's sleeve, pulling him aside. Emma tried not to eavesdrop but couldn't help overhearing snippets of their hushed conversation.

"Giuseppe, please," Valentina whispered. "Don't do it. It's dangerous."

Giuseppe shook his head. "I'll be fine. Trust me."

"But what if-"

"Shh," Giuseppe cut her off, placing a finger on Valentina's lips and glancing quickly at Emma and Daniel. "Take your guests on their tour. I'll be all right. I promise."

Emma averted her gaze, pretending to be fascinated by a nearby building. Daniel, apparently oblivious to the exchange, was busy taking photos of the canal.

Valentina rejoined them, her smile back in place, though it didn't quite reach her eyes. "Ready for your tour?"

Emma nodded, trying to push away her curiosity about the whispered conversation. "Absolutely. We can't wait to see Venice from the water."

Emma leaned back in the gondola, feeling the gentle sway as Valentina guided them through the narrow canals. The sun warmed her face, and she took a deep breath, willing away the lingering queasiness in her stomach.

She watched in fascination as Valentina maneuvered the gondola with graceful precision. The young gondolier stood at the stern of the sleek black vessel. With one foot planted firmly on the small platform at the back, Valentina propelled the boat through the water.

Her long, single oar glided so gracefully through the water that it barely disturbed the surface. Valentina's hands gripped her wooden oar with practiced ease, twisting and angling it, alternating between forward strokes and backward ones, maintaining a smooth, steady rhythm.

"Tell me about your boat," Daniel said.

"I'm so glad you asked!" Valentina said. "The term has been in use since the 11th century! Although, I believe the original boats were Roman-made and quite a bit wider than our gondolas today. As you can see, we have no cars in this part of Venice- no roads either- only canals and walkways. So the gondola is how we move about the city. We use boats for everything in Venice- trash collection, grocery delivery, visiting our neighbors, and of course, seeing the beautiful city."

Emma smiled. "I could get used to this."

"Most gondolas are eleven meters long. I believe that's about thirty-six feet, as you say in America. And they weigh nearly 360 kilos."

Daniel whistled. "I guess you're not portaging that!"

Valentina tipped her head. "What is portaging?"

While Daniel explained how people in the Great Lakes area carry their canoes between lakes by tipping them upside town and lifting them over their heads, Emma had her phone out capturing the beautiful rose and lemon-colored buildings and candy cane striped poles where people apparently tied their boats right at the doors of their houses. She marveled at the doors that opened right onto the water- "water doors," Valentina called them.

Valentina shook her head and said, "No. We will not be portaging our gondolas. Also, there is no need, since the waterways are all connected!"

As they approached a low bridge, Valentina called out, "*Abbassarsi!*" Emma and Daniel ducked their heads instinctively as they glided under the bridge, though there was plenty of clearance. The gondola glided under the stone arch without missing a beat.

At a sharp turn in the canal, Valentina dipped the oar deep into the water on one side, using it as a pivot. Then with a swift, powerful motion, she swung the gondola around, narrowly missing the weathered brick walls on either side.

Emma let out a breath she hadn't known she was holding when the gondola missed the wall and marveled at how Valentina made it all look so effortless. The gondolier's eyes cheerfully scanned the water ahead, anticipating other boats and obstacles. When they encountered another boat in a particularly narrow passage, Valentina called out to the other gondolier in Italian. They executed a graceful pass, their boats sliding past each other with mere inches to spare.

As they emerged into a wider canal, Valentina's strokes became longer and more powerful. The gondola picked up speed, cutting through the water with barely a ripple.

"How long have you been a gondolier?" Emma asked, watching as they glided past weathered brick buildings with colorful window boxes.

Valentina smiled. "Five years now. It wasn't easy breaking into this profession as a woman."

Emma nodded. "I can imagine. I own a bakery back home, and sometimes I still get people surprised to see a woman running the business."

"A fellow entrepreneur!" Valentina's eyes lit up. "What kind of bakery?"

"It's called Northern Pines Bakery. We specialize in cinnamon rolls, homemade cookies, and pastries."

Daniel chimed in, "Her cinnamon rolls are to die for."

Emma felt a small wave of nausea at the thought of food but pushed it aside. "What made you want to become a gondolier?"

Valentina steered them around a corner, revealing a picturesque bridge arching over the canal. "I've always loved the water. My father was a fisherman, and I grew up on boats. In 2010 Venice got our first female gondolier, Giorgia Boscolo, and I knew that was what I wanted to do."

"That's amazing," Emma said, genuinely impressed. "Was your family supportive?"

Valentina laughed. "Not at first. My brothers, and half the city, thought I was crazy. But I'm stubborn."

"I know that feeling," Emma grinned, then quickly covered her mouth as another wave of queasiness hit.

Daniel squeezed her hand. "You okay, honey?"

Emma nodded, forcing a smile. "Just admiring the view."

Valentina pointed to a grand building ahead. "That's the Doge's Palace. It was the residence of the Doge of Venice, the supreme authority of the former Republic."

As they approached, Emma marveled at the intricate Gothic architecture. "It's breathtaking," she said.

"How about you?" Valentina asked. "What challenges did you face starting your bakery?"

Emma thought for a moment. "Well, there was the usual stuff - securing loans, finding the right location. But the biggest challenge was probably proving myself in a small town where everyone knew each other, and I was the outsider."

Valentina nodded knowingly. "I understand that. It's not easy being the newcomer, especially when you're trying to do something different."

"Exactly," Emma agreed. "But it's worth it, isn't it? To follow your passion?"

"Absolutely," Valentina said, her smile genuine as she looked across the water. "Even on the toughest days, I wouldn't trade this for anything."

For a second, Emma thought Valentina looked sad. Or was it worried? Then the look was gone, and Valentina pointed out a small landing spot. "My favorite gelateria is just up that *calle*," she said with a smile, and Emma was sure the unhappy expression had been only her imagination.

As they drifted under another bridge, Emma felt proud of Valentina. Despite their different backgrounds, and growing up on different sides of the globe, they shared the experience of carving out their own paths in male-dominated fields.

They stopped, and Emma's head swam as she stepped off Valentina's gondola near the bustling Rialto Bridge. The market's vibrant colors and cacophony of voices overwhelmed her senses. Daniel steadied her with a gentle hand on her back.

"You sure you're up for this?" he asked.

Emma nodded. "It's the last stop of the day. I'll be fine. Let's explore."

They wove through the crowd, past stalls brimming with fresh produce, fish, cheeses, wines, aromatic spices, and glittering Venetian masks. Sellers shouted, tourists and locals filled the market, and birds swooped down trying to snatch fish from the stalls.

As they stepped into the open-air market admiring a display of fresh peaches, a booming voice startled them.

"Well, I'll be! Fellow Americans!"

They turned to see a portly man in a garish Hawaiian shirt and cargo shorts, his thinning gray hair barely contained under a "I 'HEART' Venice" cap.

"Bob Thompson, from Ohio," he announced, thrusting out his hand. "First time in Venice. Ain't it something?"

Daniel shook Bob's hand. "Daniel Lindberg, and this is Emma Harper. We're from Minnesota."

"Minnesota! Land of 10,000 lakes. Did you know Venice has 150 canals and 400 bridges? Fascinating stuff!"

Emma smiled and nodded at the American before she asked how much the peaches were. She pulled out her purse to pay for them as the woman behind the stall placed several peaches into a bag for her.

"Have you ever been anyplace like this?" Bob asked in a voice so loud that Emma winced. Without waiting for an answer, Bob said, "Of course not! Because there *is* no place else like Venice!"

Emma smiled weakly. The heat and fish smells were getting to her and her head was spinning.

As she and Daniel walked along the sidewalk, Bob followed, chatting nonstop. Emma stopped at a small display of Venetian glass. She set down her bag of peaches to steady herself against the glass shop's table.

Bob was saying something about Venetian history, his fanny pack bouncing as he gesticulated wildly. Emma nodded politely, barely registering his words.

"Well, I'm off to explore the *calles*. That means *streets* in Venetian!" Bob waved a hefty hand and grinned as he turned and headed down the steps of the bridge.

Emma waved Bob a weak farewell."

"Are you sure you're ok?" Daniel pulled her into a hug and Emma closed her eyes, her head resting against his chest. "I'll be fine. I'm glad this is our last stop. Let's find Valentina." She grabbed her bag, and they headed back to Valentina's gondola.

As they settled into the boat, Emma realized there had been a mistake. The bag that should have held several peaches felt lighter, and when she looked inside, the peaches she'd bought were missing. There were only a couple of books and a water bottle in this bag.

"Oh no," she groaned. "I grabbed the wrong bag at the glass shop."

Daniel frowned. "Should we go back?"

Emma shook her head, fatigue washing over her. "I'm beat. It was just peaches. We can get more another time. Let's head back to the hotel. I'll look through the bag when we get there and see if I can find the owner's information."

They glided in silence back through the canals to the bakery and hotel. Emma closed her eyes and wished, once again, that she'd trusted her instincts and not eaten the fish at that little place in Vicenza.

Valentina steered the gondola to the small dock behind Pasticceria Ricci. As they approached, Emma felt a wave of relief wash over her. The queasiness that had plagued her all day seemed to intensify with each passing moment.

"Here we are," Valentina announced, her voice tinged with concern. "Let me help you, Emma."

Emma nodded gratefully as Valentina steadied the boat against the dock. With surprising strength, the gondolier grasped Emma's arm and guided her onto solid ground. Emma's legs wobbled slightly as she found her footing.

"*Grazie*, Valentina," Emma managed, forcing a smile.

Daniel hopped onto the dock, the bag clutched in his hand. "Thanks for everything, Valentina. It was a great tour."

Valentina's eyes darted between them, a flicker of worry crossing her face. "Are you sure you'll be alright, Emma? There is a pharmacy up the canal. Perhaps I should-"

"We'll be fine," Daniel interjected, wrapping an arm around Emma's waist. "Nothing a good night's rest won't fix."

Emma leaned into Daniel's support, grateful for his steadying presence. She waved weakly to Valentina as Daniel guided her towards the bakery's back door.

The ancient wooden door creaked open, revealing the cozy interior of Pasticceria Ricci. The familiar scent of sugar and butter enveloped them, momentarily distracting Emma from her discomfort. The smells of a bakery reminded her of home, and she would have given almost anything to be in her own bed right then.

"Come on," Daniel urged gently, leading her through the kitchen. "Let's get you upstairs."

They hurried past gleaming copper pots and marble countertops dusted with flour. Emma caught a glimpse of Lucia's concerned face as they passed, but she didn't have the energy to stop and explain.

The narrow staircase seemed to stretch endlessly before her. Emma gripped the railing, her knuckles white as she took each step deliberately. Daniel hovered close behind, the bag clutched in one hand, ready to catch her if she faltered.

When reached the second floor, Emma fumbled with her room key, her hands shaking slightly. Daniel gently took it from her and unlocked the door, ushering her inside.

"I'll be fine," Emma said. "I just need to sleep."

"You sure?"

Emma nodded. "Positive."

As Daniel left, Emma collapsed onto the bed. It had been a wonderful day. Truly. the nausea was something every traveler dealt with at some point. She closed her eyes and rested.

Sometime later, Emma awoke, still fully clothed, lying on the bedspread. She sat up and blinked in the darkness.

The bag sat beside her. She dumped out the contents: a tourist guidebook of Venice, a water bottle, and a worn leather-bound notebook.

Hoping to find the owner's information, she flipped open the notebook. To her surprise, pages of handwritten recipes filled its interior, and at first she was delighted. Were these traditional Venetian recipes? What a rare find this might be! But as she scanned them, her brow furrowed in confusion. They were in English, not Italian. And they were not actually recipes for anything Emma would ever want to make.

Daniel knocked on her door and she called for him to come in.

"Want me to get you something for dinner?"

She smiled at him. "I'm feeling a bit better, but no. Thank you." Motioning to the notebook, she said, "This notebook that was in that bag. It's full of..." she flipped the pages, "the weirdest recipes I've ever seen."

Daniel peered over her shoulder. "Maybe you're just too tired to make sense of it."

Emma yawned. "You're probably right. I should get ready for bed and sleep for real. Although a short nap was lovely."

"You are lovely," Daniel said. "And Definitely," he agreed, gently taking the notebook from her hands. "We'll figure it out later. For now, travel exhaustion and food poisoning are combining to wipe you out. You need sleep."

Emma wanted to protest, her mind was floating with questions about the strange recipes and how to get the notebook back to its owner. But despite her nap, exhaustion won out, and she nodded reluctantly.

"Okay," she conceded as Daniel tiptoed out and shut the door. "But tomorrow we should try to get this back to its owner."

Chapter 3

E mma stirred her cappuccino, watching the foam swirl. The notebook lay on the table between her and Daniel, its worn leather cover dark against the crisp white tablecloth.

"I've looked through it twice," she said. "No name, no address, nothing. Just weird recipes, some numbers- maybe European phone numbers? - written at the bottom of each page. And on the last page, there's a graph, kind of like the ones we used to make in geometry class in high school."

Daniel took a bite of his *cornetto*. "If you think it's valuable, maybe we should turn it in to the police."

Emma shook her head. "I don't think it's valuable, really. But it feels... important. Like whoever lost it must surely want it back. I mean, who would go to the bother of writing all those odd recipes? I'd like to find the owner myself. If only to ask about the recipes."

The bell above the pasticceria's door chimed as a group of tourists entered, their excited chatter filling the room. Lucia bustled over to greet them, her spotless apron swaying.

"*Buongiorno*! Welcome, welcome. What can I get you?"

Emma watched as the tourists pointed at the display case, oohing and aahing over the colorful array of pastries.

"Those recipes," she lowered her voice, leaning towards Daniel. "They're not normal recipes. The ingredients, the instructions... it's just... weird."

Daniel raised an eyebrow. "Weird how? What do you mean?"

Before Emma could answer, a local woman in a tailored suit swept in, calling out loudly to Lucia. "The usual, *per favore*!"

Lucia nodded, already reaching for an espresso cup. "Coming right up, Signora Bianchi!"

Emma shrugged. "I think we should ask Valentina to take us back to the Rialto Bridge. Maybe we can find the owner there."

Daniel hesitated. "Are you sure you're up for it? You were pretty wiped out yesterday."

"I'm feeling much better," Emma insisted. She glanced out the window, where sunlight streamed through the vibrant bougainvillea framing the view. "It's too beautiful a day to waste," she said with a smile.

Lucia approached their table, wiping her hands on her apron. "Everything okay, my dears?"

Emma nodded. "It's perfect, Lucia. But we were wondering if you could call Valentina for us again. We need to go back to the Rialto Bridge."

Lucia's eyes twinkled. "Of course! Isn't the market amazing? Let me get my phone." She paused, looking at the notebook. "What's that you've got there? A recipe book?"

Emma hesitated. "Actually, Lucia, maybe you might take a look at it. It's full of recipes, but... well, they don't quite make sense to me."

Emma watched as Lucia flipped through the notebook, her brow furrowing as she scanned the pages. The bakery hummed with activity around them, but Emma was waiting for Lucia's reaction.

"Hmm," Lucia muttered, pausing to read a particular page more closely. She shook her head, salt-and-pepper curls bouncing. "You're right, *cara*. These aren't proper recipes at all."

Emma leaned forward. "What do you think they are? Fish and vanilla in the same recipe? And look at this one." Emma flipped a few pages. "*Roll the butter in dough and bring it to the books*. What on earth?"

Lucia shrugged, her flour-dusted hands leaving faint marks on the leather cover as she closed the notebook. "Could be a child's game, perhaps? Or someone pretending to write recipes without knowing how." She handed the notebook back to Emma. "It certainly makes not much sense to me."

Emma took the notebook. "Well, thank you for looking," she said, tucking the notebook into her bag.

Lucia patted Emma's hand. "Of course, dear. Now, let me call Valentina for you. I'm sure she'd be happy to take you back to the Rialto Bridge."

As Lucia bustled off to make the call, Emma turned to Daniel. "What do you think? Should we still try to find the owner?"

Daniel nodded, finishing the last bite of his *cornetto*. "It can't hurt to look. And if nothing else, it'll be another chance to explore the city."

Emma smiled, feeling a surge of affection for Daniel's support. She was grateful he didn't dismiss her curiosity about the notebook, even if it was a trivial mystery. It was one of the things she loved about him. He supported her in whatever hair-brained idea she had. She couldn't imagine her life without him.

Emma set the bag with the leather-bound notebook between her feet as Valentina's gondola glided through the narrow canals. The gentle lapping of water against stone echoed off the weathered buildings, their pastel facades reflected in the deep green of the canal.

"There it is," Emma pointed as the Rialto Bridge came into view. "Can you drop us off near that glass shop?"

Valentina nodded, expertly maneuvering the gondola to a nearby dock. As they disembarked, Emma noticed the gondolier's furrowed brow.

"Everything okay, Valentina?" she asked.

Valentina forced a smile. "Just worried about Giuseppe. He didn't show up for work this morning."

Emma gave the gondolier a concerned look. "I hope he's ok."

Valentina nodded. "He's probably home sick. But I wish he would answer my calls."

"Being sick is the worst," Emma said with true empathy. "I hope he gets better soon."

At the glass shop where she'd accidentally picked up the bag, Emma approached the counter. A middle-aged woman was arranging delicate figurines.

"Excuse me," Emma began, "I was here yesterday afternoon, and accidentally took the wrong bag. I'm trying to find the owner of the notebook that was inside." She held up the bag. "Has anyone come asking for it?"

The woman shook her head with a frown. "No, *signora*. No one has asked about a notebook."

Emma pulled it out and showed it to the woman. "Is it yours, by any chance?"

The woman shook her head. "Not mine."

Emma's shoulders slumped. "Thank you anyway."

They tried the fish market next, weaving through crowds of shoppers examining glistening displays of seafood. The air was thick with the briny scent of the sea and the shouts of vendors.

"Any luck?" Daniel asked as Emma returned from questioning a burly fishmonger.

She shook her head. "Nothing. Let's try the produce market."

But as before, among the colorful stalls piled high with fruits and vegetables, no one recognized the notebook or knew of anyone searching for it.

Emma sighed, leaning against a stone pillar. "I really thought we'd find the owner. It's such a cool notebook, bound in leather, and the contents are so... interesting. I figured someone would be looking for it."

Daniel squeezed her shoulder. "You tried your best. Maybe we can turn it in to the police later. Although I think Lucia's probably right. It was someone doodling, having fun making things up. Probably a child's book to keep them busy on a family vacation."

Emma nodded as they made their way back to Valentina. "I guess you're right. It's just a notebook. And I'm just a baker interested in crazy recipes. I don't think it's worth bothering the police. I'm sure they have more important things to take care of than some tourist's notebook."

Valentina hurried toward them, her phone in hand. "I hate to cut this short, but I'm going to head to Murano to check on Giuseppe. He is still not answering, and his neighbor has also not seen him last night or today. I'm getting worried."

Emma perked up. "Murano? Isn't that where the famous glass blowers are?"

Valentina nodded. "Yes, it's beautiful. I could take you there by *vaporetto* if you'd like. My boyfriend works at one of the workshops. You can have a look around while I check on Giuseppe."

"*Vaporetto*?" Daniel asked, his brow furrowed.

"It's like a water bus," Valentina explained. "Much faster than a gondola for longer trips."

Emma and Daniel exchanged smiles. "That sounds great," Emma said. "We'd love to see the glass blowers."

They made their way to the nearest *vaporetto* stop, a wooden platform jutting out into the canal. A small crowd had already gathered, a mix of locals and tourists chattering in various languages. Emma clutched her bag with the mysterious notebook to her chest and remembered the conversation she'd overheard yesterday as they were waiting for another boat ride- their first ride in Valentina's gondola. Valentina had asked Giuseppe not to do something, and he had assured her he would be fine.

Was his absence today connected to the conversation yesterday?

The platform swayed gently under her feet as they waited. Emma leaned against the railing, watching the sparkle of sunlight on the water, and tried not to think about Giuseppe being in any sort of trouble. This was, as Daniel had said, a vacation. She turned as she heard the low rumble of an approaching engine from a distance.

"Here it comes," Valentina said, pointing to a sleek white vessel rounding the bend.

The *vaporetto* was larger than Emma had imagined, but it cut through the water with surprising grace. Its wake sent small waves lapping against the dock. As it drew closer, Emma could make out the passengers inside, some seated, others standing near the exits.

The boat slowed, maneuvering alongside the platform with practiced ease. A deckhand tossed a rope to secure it, and the doors slid open. A flood of passengers disembarked, creating a momentary crush of bodies.

"Ready?" Daniel asked, placing a hand on Emma's back.

They joined the line of people waiting to board. Emma felt the gentle push of bodies as they shuffled forward. The interior of the *vaporetto* was utilitarian but clean, with rows of plastic seats and large windows offering panoramic views of the canal.

Emma, Daniel, and Valentina found seats near the back, settling in as the last passengers boarded. With a low rumble, the vaporetto pulled away from the dock, Venice's ancient buildings sliding past as they set off across open water towards the nearby island of Murano.

Emma's eyes widened as Murano came into view. The island's skyline, dotted with church spires and colorful buildings, reflected in the shimmering water. As they neared the dock, she spotted rows of shops with glittering displays in their windows.

"Oh. It's beautiful," Emma breathed, leaning towards Daniel.

He nodded, squeezing her hand. "Like a postcard come to life."

The *vaporetto* bumped gently against the dock. Emma followed Valentina and Daniel off the boat, her legs wobbling slightly as she walked the last few feet off the boat.

"Marco's workshop is just down this way," Valentina said, gesturing down a narrow street lined with shops.

As they walked, Emma's gaze darted from window to window, each one filled with dazzling glass creations. Delicate flowers, vibrant vases, and intricate figurines caught the sunlight, casting rainbow reflections on the cobblestones.

"Look at that!" Emma tugged on Daniel's sleeve, pointing to a massive chandelier hanging in one shop window. Its crystal drops sparkled like a frozen waterfall.

"Incredible," Daniel murmured. "I can't imagine how long that must have taken to make."

They rounded a corner, and Valentina led them to a weathered wooden door. A small sign above read "*Fornace della Fenice*" in elegant script.

"It means *Furnace of the Phoenix*," Valentina said as she pushed the door open. When they stepped inside, she called out, "Marco? Are you here?"

A tall man with tousled black hair emerged from the back, wiping his hands on a cloth. His face lit up when he saw Valentina.

"Val! I wasn't expecting you today." He gave her a quick kiss, then turned to Emma and Daniel. "And who are your friends?"

"This is Emma and Daniel," Valentina said. "They're visiting from America. I thought they might like to see a real Murano glass workshop."

Marco's green eyes crinkled as he smiled. "Welcome! I'd be happy to show you around." He glanced at Valentina. "Everything okay? You look worried."

Valentina bit her lip. "I need to check on Giuseppe. He didn't show up for work, and I can't reach him. Would you mind giving Emma and Daniel the tour while I go to his place?"

Marco nodded, his expression turning serious. "Of course. Let me know if you need anything." He stepped toward her and more quietly said, "Be careful."

As Valentina hurried out, Marco turned to Emma and Daniel. "Shall we begin the tour? I was just about to start a new piece."

Emma's eyes widened as Marco led them into the heart of his workshop. The heat hit her like a wall, and she felt beads of sweat form on her forehead. The air shimmered with an intense, dry warmth that made her throat feel parched.

"This is where the magic happens," Marco said, gesturing to the glowing furnaces. "We keep these burning at around 2,000 degrees Fahrenheit."

Emma watched, mesmerized, as Marco gathered a glob of molten glass on the end of a long metal pipe. The glass glowed a brilliant orange, reminding her of the embers of a dying fire.

"Murano has been famous for glassmaking since the 13th century," Marco explained as he rolled the pipe, shaping the glass. "The Venetian government moved all the glassmakers here to protect the secrets of our trade."

He dipped the glowing mass into a container of colored glass chips, then returned it to the furnace. Emma caught a whiff of something acrid and metallic as Marco worked.

"Those are metal oxides," he said, noticing her wrinkled nose. "They give the glass its color."

Emma's gaze wandered to the shelves lining the walls. Delicate vases in swirling patterns of blue and green stood next to abstract sculptures that seemed to defy gravity. A collection of tiny glass animals caught her eye - each one perfectly formed, from the curve of a dolphin's tail to the proud stance of a miniature lion.

"This piece will be a vase," Marco said, bringing her attention back to his work. He blew gently into the pipe, and Emma watched in awe as the glass expanded like a balloon.

Using tools that looked like giant tweezers and scissors, Marco shaped the vase, his movements fluid and precise. The glass shifted from orange to a deep, rich red as it cooled.

"The color will deepen even more as it cools completely," he explained.

Emma felt a tug of inspiration as she watched Marco work. The artistry, the history, the sheer skill involved - it reminded her of her own passion for baking. Different mediums, but the same devotion to craft.

Emma was transfixed as Marco continued to shape the vase. His hands moved with practiced grace, coaxing the molten glass into a swirling circle of color. The deep red glass twisted and turned, creating patterns that reminded Emma of autumn leaves caught in a whirlpool.

Daniel leaned in close, his eyes wide with wonder. "It's like he's painting with fire," he whispered to Emma.

She nodded, unable to tear her gaze away from Marco's work. The heat from the furnace made her skin prickle, but she barely noticed, too engrossed in the artistry unfolding before her.

As Marco put the finishing touches on the vase, he glanced up at them with a smile. "Now, let me show you where we display our finished pieces."

He led them to the front of the Fornace della Fenice, where a three-story shop showcased an array of breathtaking glasswork. Emma's jaw dropped as they entered the space. Sunlight streamed through large windows, making the glass creations sparkle and dance.

"This is incredible," Emma breathed, her eyes darting from one piece to another.

They walked slowly among the displays, admiring the intricate details of each creation. A glass saxophone caught Emma's eye, its brass color so realistic she almost expected to hear music when she looked at it.

"That piece is meant to represent music," Marco explained, noticing her interest. "The way the light plays off the curves is meant to mimic the flow of a melody."

As they moved through the shop, Emma spotted a collection of vases like the one Marco had been making. Each one was unique, with swirling patterns in various shades of red, blue, and green.

Daniel asked Marco how he learned to create art from glass.

Emma listened as Marco began to share his journey into the world of glassblowing. His green eyes sparkled with passion as he spoke, reminding her of the way she felt when talking about her own bakery.

"I grew up here on Murano," Marco began, his voice warm with nostalgia. "As a child, I'd spend hours watching the maestros work through the windows of their workshops. It was like magic to me."

Emma nodded, understanding the allure of watching skilled artisans at work. She thought of her own childhood fascination with watching bakers create intricate pastries.

Marco continued, "When I was fourteen, my uncle offered me an apprenticeship at his workshop. I jumped at the chance." He chuckled, shaking his head. "Those first few years were tough. I burned myself more times than I can count, and I broke so many pieces I thought I'd never get it right."

Emma winced sympathetically, remembering her own early struggles with baking. "But you didn't give up," she said, admiration clear in her voice.

"No, I didn't," Marco agreed. "There's something about working with glass that gets under your skin. The way it moves, how it responds to heat and breath - it's alive in a way that's hard to describe."

He led them to a display case filled with intricate figurines. "These were some of my first successful pieces," he said, pointing to a collection of small animals. "I spent months perfecting the technique to make them."

Emma leaned in, marveling at the delicate details of a tiny glass elephant. Its trunk was curled upward, and she could almost see the wrinkles in its skin.

"As I got better, I started experimenting with different techniques and colors," Marco explained. "I traveled to other parts of Italy and even to Germany to learn from different masters. Each place had its own unique style and methods."

Emma noticed the way Marco's hands moved as he spoke, as if he were shaping invisible glass in the air. It reminded her of the way she often found herself mimicking kneading motions when talking about bread.

"Now," Marco said, his voice filled with pride, "I have my own workshop, and I get to create pieces that are shipped all over the world. But more importantly, I get to keep this ancient tradition alive and pass it on to the next generation."

Emma was about to ask Marco about his favorite piece when the shop's door burst open. Valentina rushed in, her face pale and eyes wide with shock.

"Marco," she gasped, her voice trembling. "It's Giuseppe. He's... he's dead."

The room fell silent as Marco rushed forward, gripping Valentina's shoulders. "What? How?"

Valentina shook her head. "They found him here in Murano, in the canal by his house this morning. I don't know what happened. The police are everywhere. They won't let me into his house."

Emma exchanged a worried glance with Daniel. She remembered again the whispered conversation between Valentina and Giuseppe at the dock and Giuseppe assuring Valentina he'd be fine. Clearly, he wasn't.

Marco pulled Valentina into a tight embrace. "Oh my dear, I'm so sorry," he murmured.

Emma felt like an intruder on their grief. She cleared her throat softly. "Is there anything we can do to help?"

Valentina pulled away from Marco, wiping her eyes. "No, I... I don't think so. I just needed to tell Marco. The police want to speak with me." She looked up at Marco. "You can come with me?"

"Of course," he whispered. "Of course."

Emma and Daniel stepped toward the door. "We can leave. You'll need some time alone."

Marco nodded. "I need to close up the shop and go with Valentina to speak with the police. You can take the *vaporetto* back to Venice? You know the way?"

"Yes, of course," Daniel said. "Is there anything we can get for you, Valentina? Do you need a drink, or anything?"

She shook her head, her eyes filling with tears again.

As Marco moved to lock the front door, Emma remembered Giuseppe's cheerful smile, his kind eyes. What, she wondered, had Valentina warned him against doing?

"Valentina," Emma said gently, "I'm so sorry about Giuseppe. He seemed like a wonderful person."

Valentina nodded, her tears spilling down her cheeks. "He was. I can't believe..." She trailed off, her gaze darting to Marco.

Emma noticed the silent exchange between them, a flicker of something more than grief passing between their eyes. She wanted to ask more, to understand what was really going on, but she held back. This wasn't the time or place.

Emma watched as Marco held Valentina as they walked together up the canal into the heart of Murano.

Emma and Daniel slowly made their way back through the narrow streets of Murano, passing colorful glass shops now dulled by the somber mood. As they approached the dock for the water taxi, Emma's eyes were drawn to a commotion up the street. A group of police officers huddled together, their voices low and urgent.

"Look," Emma nudged Daniel, pointing discreetly. "There's Valentina and Marco."

The young Italian couple walked toward the gathered officers, their faces etched with worry. Emma felt a pang of sympathy, mixed with an unsettling sense of unease.

"I was hoping for a vacation without any murders," Emma sighed, her voice barely above a whisper.

Daniel squeezed her hand. "We don't know that it was a murder, Emma. Let's not jump to conclusions."

Emma bit her lip, hesitating for a moment before speaking. "But he was found dead in a canal. And also, there's something I overheard. When we first met Valentina, while you were taking pictures in the gondola, I overheard her talking to Giuseppe. She told him not to do something, that it was too dangerous."

Daniel's brow furrowed. "That doesn't sound good." He looked back up the street to the group of police. "What do you think she was referring to?"

"I don't know, but I'm afraid she might have been right. About whatever it was." Emma's stomach churned, and not from the lingering effects of her food poisoning.

As they stepped onto the dock, the *vaporetto* glided into view, its engine humming softly against the lapping waves. Emma cast one last glance at Valentina and Marco, now speaking with the police. Valentina was shaking her head vehemently, her long hair blowing in the breeze.

The weight of the young man's death sat heavy in Emma's chest as they boarded the *vaporetto*. As the boat pulled away from Murano, she watched the famous island shrink in the distance, her mind swirling with questions.

Chapter 4

Emma flopped onto the bed in Daniel's room, her stomach growling. "I'm starving. Let's get pizza."

Daniel raised an eyebrow. "We're right on the sea. How about some fresh fish?"

Emma wrinkled her nose. "Fish? After what happened last time?" She threw a pillow across the room at him.

He caught it and raised his eyebrows at her. "That was days ago. You're feeling better now, right?"

"Yeah, but..." Emma trailed off as she rolled over, realizing her irritation wasn't just about food. Giuseppe's death weighed on her mind. The thought of food felt trivial in comparison, but her growling stomach demanded attention.

Daniel sat beside her and set the pillow back at the head of the bed.

Oblivious to her inner turmoil, he continued his culinary pitch. "Or we could get pasta. I know we're in Italy, but I'm just not feeling like pizza right now. How about that little trattoria we passed near the Rialto? The one with the red awning? I bet they have amazing carbonara."

Emma rolled onto her side, facing away from him. "I just want something simple and familiar."

"Familiar? We're in Venice! This is our chance to try real Italian cuisine." Daniel's enthusiasm grated on her nerves. "Remember that place by the canal? With the outdoor seating? I saw someone eating the most incredible-looking seafood linguine."

"Daniel, please," Emma groaned, pulling a pillow over her head.

He persisted, undeterred. "Or what about that cozy spot near the Piazza San Marco? I heard they make their pasta fresh every day and use fresh seafood."

Emma sat up abruptly. "I don't care about pasta! And I don't want to even think about fish! I don't want to think about restaurants or menus or anything right now. Can't we just order in?"

Daniel blinked, taken aback by her outburst. "Hey, what's really going on?" He looked at her, suddenly aware she was actually upset. "This isn't about food, is it?"

Emma's shoulders slumped. "No, it's not. I just... Giuseppe's dead, Daniel. We were talking to him yesterday, and now he's gone. How can we sit here and debate pasta choices?"

Daniel's expression softened as understanding dawned. He moved closer, placing a gentle hand on her shoulder. "I'm sorry, Emma. I didn't realize how much this was affecting you."

Emma felt the tension in her shoulders slowly release as Daniel's hand rested there. She took a deep breath, letting Daniel's kindness relieve some of the weight of Giuseppe's death. The room fell quiet, save for the distant chatter of tourists on the street below.

After a few moments, Emma rolled over to face Daniel. His blue eyes held concern, and she felt a pang of guilt for snapping at him earlier.

"I'm sorry," she murmured. "It's just... it's hard to process. We were laughing with him yesterday, and now..."

Daniel nodded, understanding etched across his features. "I know. It's shocking. We don't have to go out if you're not up for it."

Emma sat up and leaned into him, resting her head on his shoulder. The familiar scent of his cologne brought her a small measure of comfort. They sat in silence for a while, the reality of mortality hanging heavy in the air.

As the minutes ticked by, Emma's stomach let out an audible growl. She couldn't help but let out a small chuckle.

"I guess my body has other ideas," she said, sitting up straight. "And I don't actually know if 'ordering in' is a thing in Italy. Maybe we should go find something to eat after all."

Daniel's lips quirked into a gentle smile. "Whatever you want, Em. We can see if ordering in is an option."

Emma considered for a moment, then shook her head. "No, let's go out. Maybe some fresh air will do us good." She stood up, smoothing out her shirt. "But let's keep it simple, okay? I'm not sure I'm up for a fancy sit-down meal right now."

"Simple it is," Daniel agreed, getting to his feet. "How about we just wander and see what catches our eye? No pressure, no plans."

Emma nodded, feeling a small spark of her usual enthusiasm returning. "That sounds perfect. Who knows? Maybe we'll stumble on one place that has both the best pizza and fish in Venice."

He smiled at her and they fell silent, the only sound the gentle lapping of water against the canal outside. Emma walked to the window to where she'd left her shoes.

Daniel joined her, wrapping an arm around her waist. "It'll be ok. And everything looks better on a full stomach."

Emma turned to him, their eyes meeting. Despite their disagreement, she felt a surge of affection. She leaned in, their lips meeting in a soft kiss.

Holding Daniel's hand, Emma sighed and leaned against the window frame, her eyes tracing the path of a passing gondola. The gentle lapping of water against stone soothed her frayed nerves. Daniel kissed her again, this time on her cheek, and his warmth at her side anchored her to the present moment.

"Look," Daniel said, motioning toward the window. "Isn't that Valentina?"

Emma squinted, focusing on the approaching gondola. "You're right. It is her."

Without a word, they both turned and hurried out of the room. Their footsteps echoed through the narrow stairwell as they rushed down to the *pasticceria's* back entrance.

Emma pushed open the weathered wooden door, the scent of salt water and aged wood filling her nostrils. "Valentina!" she called out, waving her arm.

Valentina's head snapped up at the sound of her name. Even from a distance, Emma could see the redness rimming her eyes. The gondolier steered her craft closer to the small dock.

"Emma, Daniel," Valentina said, her voice hoarse. "How are you both?"

Daniel stepped forward. "We saw you from our window. Are you okay?"

Valentina shook her head, a stray tear escaping down her cheek. "Not really. It's been... a difficult day."

Emma felt a pang in her chest. "We were just about to get dinner. Would you like to join us?"

Valentina hesitated, her gaze drifting to the water. "I don't know..."

"Come on," Daniel urged. "We're just getting pizza. Nothing fancy."

Emma turned to him, surprised. "Pizza?"

He shrugged, a small smile playing at his lips. "Yeah, I think you're right, it might be nice."

Emma squeezed his hand, warmth blooming in her chest. She looked back at Valentina. "What do you say? Pizza and company might help take your mind off things for a bit."

Valentina seemed to consider for a moment before nodding slowly. "Okay. Thank you. I... I think I'd like that."

As Valentina secured her gondola, Emma leaned into Daniel. "Thanks for agreeing to pizza," she whispered.

He wrapped an arm around her waist. "Of course. And hey, maybe we can do fish or pasta tomorrow night?"

Emma nodded, grateful for his understanding. "Absolutely. It's a date."

Emma's stomach growled as they walked along the narrow Venetian streets. The aroma of vinegars, flavored oils, and simmering sauces wafted from nearby restaurants, making her mouth water.

"I think I know a good place," Valentina said, leading them through a maze of alleys. "It's off the beaten path, but the pizza is amazing."

As they rounded a corner, Emma spotted a familiar figure ahead. "Is that...?"

Bob turned around and spotted them, his face lighting up. "Well, if it isn't my favorite Venetian explorers!" He ambled over, his Hawaiian shirt a riot of colors in the fading light.

"Heading to dinner?" Emma asked.

Bob pulled off his "I Heart Venice" baseball cap and fanned himself with it as he nodded enthusiastically. "You betcha! Found this little place that serves something called 'pizza al taglio.' Sounds fancy!"

Valentina chuckled. "It just means pizza by the slice."

"Oh." Bob's face fell for a moment before brightening again. "Well, when in Rome! Or Venice, I guess."

He waved farewell and hurried up the street as they continued on their way. Soon, Valentina led them into a small *campo*, or square, where a quaint pizzeria nestled in the corner. Twinkling lights hung overhead, casting a warm glow on the handful of outdoor tables.

"This is perfect," Emma said as they settled into their seats.

A waiter appeared, and after discussing what they'd like, Valentina ordered for them in rapid Italian. As they waited for their food, Emma noticed Valentina's gaze darting around nervously.

"Valentina," Emma said softly, "are you okay?"

Valentina's eyes snapped to Emma's face. She opened her mouth, then closed it again, shaking her head.

Daniel leaned in. "Giuseppe?"

Valentina's shoulders slumped. "Yes," she whispered. "But I don't think I should talk about it right now."

Emma's mouth watered as the waiter approached their table, balancing three steaming pizzas on a large wooden board. The aroma of fresh basil, melted mozzarella, and wood-fired crust filled the air.

"Grazie," Valentina murmured as the waiter set the board down, the pizzas sizzling invitingly.

Emma's eyes widened at the sight. The crust was thin and perfectly charred around the edges, the toppings vibrant and fresh. She reached for a slice of margherita, the classic combination of tomato, mozzarella, and basil calling to her.

As she took her first bite, Emma couldn't help but close her eyes in delight. The flavors exploded on her tongue, the crust crisp yet chewy, the tomatoes bursting with sweetness.

"This is incredible," she said, opening her eyes to see Daniel nodding in agreement, his mouth full.

The small campo was bathed in the warm glow of sunset, casting long shadows across the cobblestones. Their table, the only one occupied in the outdoor seating area, felt intimate and cozy. A gentle breeze rustled the leaves of a nearby tree, bringing welcome relief from the day's heat.

Emma poured sparkling water into their glasses, the bubbles catching the fading light. She glanced at Valentina, who was picking at her pizza, her eyes distant.

"So, Marco's workshop was fascinating," Emma said, hoping to draw Valentina into the conversation. "I've never seen anything like it. The way he shaped that vase was like magic."

Daniel nodded enthusiastically. "The colors he used were incredible. I had no idea glass could look like that."

Valentina smiled faintly. "Yes, Marco is very talented. He comes from a long line of Murano glassblowers."

But even as she spoke, Emma noticed Valentina's gaze drifting, her thoughts clearly elsewhere. Emma exchanged a concerned look with Daniel, unsure how to comfort their new friend in the wake of Giuseppe's death.

Emma watched Valentina push her pizza around her plate, barely taking a bite. The gondolier's eyes were distant, her thoughts clearly elsewhere. Emma reached out and gently touched Valentina's hand.

"Valentina, would you like to tell us about Giuseppe? How did you two meet?"

Valentina's eyes refocused, a small smile tugging at her lips. "We met during training, actually. Giuseppe was always making jokes, trying to lighten the mood when things got tough."

Emma nodded encouragingly. "How long have you worked together?"

"Almost three years now." Valentina's smile grew. "Giuseppe had this way of charming even the grumpiest tourists. He'd sing old Venetian songs, tell the corniest jokes. But people loved it."

As Valentina spoke, her eyes lit up with fond memories. "There was this one time, during Carnival. Giuseppe showed up in the most ridiculous mask I've ever seen. It was shaped like a giant fish, with glittery scales and bulging eyes. He wore it all day, claiming it was 'good for business.'" She laughed softly. "Surprisingly, it was. We had more customers that day than ever before."

Emma smiled, glad to see Valentina's mood lifting. But as quickly as it had come, the light in Valentina's eyes dimmed. She fell silent, her gaze dropping to her untouched pizza.

Suddenly, a group of boisterous tourists walked by their table, laughing loudly. Valentina startled, her head snapping up, eyes wide with fear.

After the group had passed into a narrow *calle*, or alleyway, Daniel leaned forward, his brow furrowed with concern. "Valentina, is there something more than missing Giuseppe that's weighing on you?"

Valentina shook her head quickly, avoiding their eyes. "No, no. It's nothing. I'm just... I'm just sad about Giuseppe."

Emma exchanged a glance with Daniel, then turned back to Valentina. "Listen, Valentina. I know we've only just met, but we want to help if we can. Daniel's a detective back home. If there's something more going on, maybe we could-"

"No," Valentina cut her off, her voice sharp. Then, more softly, "I'm sorry. I appreciate your concern, but... I can't talk about it. Not here. Not now."

"There is no one else here," Emma said. "And we are good listeners."

"I... we..." Valentina took a shaky breath. "Giuseppe and I, we had noticed some... strange things happening in the gondolier community."

Emma nodded. "What kind of strange things?"

Valentina glanced around again before continuing. "I can't talk about it. Giuseppe wanted me to. He tried to convince me to go with him, but I was scared. And now..." Her voice broke.

Emma reached across the table, squeezing Valentina's hand. "You think he talked about whatever was going on, and that's why he died." It wasn't a question.

Tears welled in Valentina's eyes. "And now, I don't know what to do. I'm afraid I'll be next."

"Valentina," Emma said urgently, "you need to tell us everything you know. We can help-"

Valentina shook her head violently. "No, I can't. It's too dangerous. I shouldn't have said anything at all." She pushed back her chair and gave them a watery smile. "Thank you for the dinner. I'm sorry my appetite is not well tonight. You can find your way back to your hotel, yes?"

When Emma nodded, reaching out a hand to Valentina, the gondolier shook her head and hurried away down the narrow *calle* and disappeared from view.

Chapter 5

E mma woke to the sound of small birds chirping in the bougainvillea outside her window. She stretched, feeling much better than she had in days. Before she could sit up, there was a knock on her door.

"Come in!"

Daniel peeked inside, then came in carrying a coffee mug. He settled himself in the chair at the small table by the window and took a sip of his coffee. "Morning, sleepyhead," he said. "What do you want to do today?"

Emma smiled at the sight of Daniel's messy hair. He'd been up long enough to get coffee from downstairs but had clearly not showered yet. Then, remembering the previous day, she bit her lip. "Maybe we could find Valentina? I'm worried about her."

Daniel sighed. "I know you want to help, but it's not our business. Valentina's a capable woman. She'll handle it."

"But what if she's in danger?" Emma protested.

"She managed to become one of the few female gondoliers in Venice. I think she can take care of herself."

Emma frowned, unconvinced. "It just doesn't feel right to ignore it."

Daniel set down his coffee and held out his hand.

She got up and went to him, nuzzling her face in his neck.

"Let's focus on our vacation," Daniel whispered. "We're here to get away from all the mysteries and stress of life, remember? We can wander the city, do some shopping. What do you say?"

Emma nodded reluctantly. "Okay. You're probably right."

They showered, dressed, and grabbed pastries from Lucia on their way out into the Venetian morning. Sunlight glittered on the water in the canals and the sky was a perfect summer blue.

As they crossed an open square with a water fountain, Emma tossed a bite of her pastry to a pigeon. Twenty other pigeons flocked around her and clearly asking for more. Emma laughed and shoed them away.

"This is my breakfast!" she laughed. "Find your own food!"

Daniel wrapped an arm around her waist and together, they walked down a shaded *calle* into a shopping district.

A gondola floated beneath them as they crossed one of the hundreds of small bridges, and Emma turned, her heart leaping. But it was not Valentina. The man guiding the gondola was burly and tanned, his eyes sharp black. Emma realized she had stopped walking to watch the boat pass and hurried to catch up with Daniel.

They spent the morning exploring Venice's winding streets and bridges. Emma tried to lose herself in the beauty of the city, but her mind kept drifting to Valentina.

Emma's eyes widened as they stepped into a small shop. Delicate glass creations hung from every surface, catching the light and throwing miniature rainbows across the walls.

"Oh, Daniel, look at these!" She pointed to a display of pendants, each containing a collection of tiny flowers made of glass.

Daniel leaned in, squinting. "How do they even make these?"

"With great skill and patience," a voice answered. The shopkeeper, a young woman with short brown hair and bright blue glasses approached them. "Each flower is crafted by hand, petal by petal."

Emma ran her finger along a row of pendants. "They're exquisite."

"They suit you," Daniel said, picking up a pendant made of dozens of delicate blue flowers inside a gold circle.

Emma's breath caught. "It's perfect."

As Daniel paid for the necklace, Emma wandered the shop, marveling at the other creations. Tiny glass balls dangled from metal teardrops, and necklaces made of vibrant twists of glass adorned mannequin necks.

"What do you think of these?" Emma asked, gesturing to a set of earrings shaped like miniature hot air balloons.

Daniel chuckled. "A bit much for everyday wear, don't you think?"

"Maybe for you," Emma teased. She turned back to the shopkeeper. "How long have you been making these?"

"Oh, I don't make them myself," the young woman replied with a laugh. "They come from Murano. I'm just a shopkeeper."

Daniel turned to Emma with the wrapped pendant and chain. "Ready?"

Emma nodded, then paused. "Actually, could you put it on me now?"

Daniel smiled and carefully fastened the chain around her neck. The pendant nestled just below her collarbone, cool against her skin.

"It's lovely on you," the shopkeeper said. "A perfect memento of Venice."

As they left the shop, Emma touched the pendant, her mind drifting back to Valentina and the mystery surrounding Giuseppe's death. She pushed the thoughts away, determined to enjoy this moment with Daniel.

Nevertheless, as they browsed a small shop selling Venetian masks, Emma noticed movement on the canal and her eyes darted outside.

"See anything you like?" Daniel asked, holding up an ornate mask of a bird with a long, pointed beak.

"Huh? Oh, yeah. It's nice," Emma said distractedly, craning her neck to see a passing gondola out the window.

Daniel followed her gaze. "You're still thinking about Valentina, aren't you?"

Emma sighed. "I can't help it. I keep looking for her every time I see a gondola."

"Do you think I look handsome as a bird doctor?"

Emma blinked, her mind snapping back from thoughts of Valentina. "Bird doctor? What are you talking about?"

Daniel grinned, still holding the long-beaked mask. "This mask. It's a plague doctor mask. They used these during outbreaks in the 16th and 17th centuries."

"Really?" Emma leaned closer, examining the mask's hollow eye sockets and elongated beak.

"Yep. Doctors would stuff the beak with herbs and spices. They thought it would purify the air and protect them from the plague."

Emma wrinkled her nose. "That's... unsettling."

"It gets better," Daniel continued, clearly enjoying the impromptu history lesson. "They'd wear these masks with long, waxed leather coats, gloves, and boots. The whole outfit was supposed to form a head-to-toe protective barrier."

Emma took a step back from the mask display. "Medieval personal protective wear. I can't imagine how terrifying it must have been to see someone dressed like that coming towards you when you were sick."

"Probably not as scary as the plague itself," Daniel mused.

Emma shuddered, eyeing the various bird-like masks lining the shelves. Their empty eyes and sharp beaks seemed to follow her. "I think I've had enough plague history for one day. Can we go?"

Daniel set the mask down, nodding. "Sure. How about we find a nice cafe for lunch?"

As they left the shop, Emma cast one last glance at the bird masks. Their eerie presence lingered in her mind, a stark reminder of Venice's complex history.

They continued their shopping, but Emma's attention remained divided. Every gondolier they passed made her heart jump, only to sink again when it wasn't Valentina.

Emma licked her gelato, savoring the creamy pistachio flavor as she and Daniel pushed open the door to Pasticceria Ricci. Her feet ached from a day of exploring Venice's winding streets, but the sweet treat helped soothe her weariness.

As they entered, the rich scent of sugar and vanilla enveloped them. Lucia stood behind the counter, her salt-and-pepper curls escaping from her loose ponytail as she vigorously whisked a bowl of egg whites.

"Ah, welcome back!" Lucia called out, her face flushed from exertion. "How was your day?"

"Exhausting," Emma admitted, collapsing onto a nearby chair. "But beautiful. What are you making?"

Lucia's eyes twinkled. "Italian meringues. For the top of a lemon tart."

Emma perked up, her fatigue momentarily forgotten. "Oh! I've always wanted to learn how to make those. Would you mind teaching me?"

Lucia beamed. "Of course! Come, wash your hands and I'll show you."

As Emma moved to the sink, Daniel settled into a chair. "I'll just watch, if you don't mind. My culinary skills are limited to microwaving leftovers."

Lucia laughed, a hearty sound that filled the small bakery. "Very well. Emma, come here and I'll show you the trick to getting the sugar syrup just right."

As Lucia explained the process, Emma found her mind wandering. The carefully measured ingredients reminded her of the leather-bound notebook hidden in her room upstairs. Those recipes were so strange, nothing like the precise instructions Lucia was giving her now.

"Emma? Are you listening?" Lucia's voice snapped her back to attention.

"Sorry, I was just thinking about..." Emma trailed off, unsure how to explain. "Never mind. You were saying about the temperature?"

Lucia nodded, returning to her explanation. But as Emma watched the sugar syrup bubble in the pot, her thoughts drifted to Valentina. Where was she now? Was she safe? The image of the young gondolier's tear-stained face from the night before haunted Emma.

"Now, we'll slowly pour this into the egg whites while whisking," Lucia instructed, lifting the pot.

Emma nodded, her hands moving mechanically as she helped with the meringue. But her heart wasn't in it. She glanced out the back window at the canal, unable to shake the feeling that Valentina was in trouble.

Chapter 6

Emma propped herself up against the headboard, the leather-bound notebook resting on her lap. The soft glow of the bedside lamp cast shadows across the pages as she flipped through them once more.

"This doesn't make any sense," she muttered, squinting at the bizarre ingredient lists. A recipe for crepes included fresh fish in the batter. On the next page, a recipe for Italian meringues included eight slices of polenta. She shook her head. Lucia had said it might be a child's attempt at writing recipes, but the handwriting was not a child's handwriting. And the leather-bound book was far too nice to have been intended as a child's plaything. But what could it mean?

Then Emma's eyes traveled to the string of numbers at the bottom of each page, handwritten in small lettering. Again, she wondered if they were European phone numbers.

Peering at them, her brow furrowed. "Three numbers, dash, three numbers, dash, three numbers, comma, and another set?" After a pause in which she considered, she whispered, "One way to find out!"

She grabbed her phone from the nightstand, punched in the first set of numbers, and hit the call button. A recording in Italian that she couldn't understand exactly let her know that was not a phone number. She tried again with another set, but still nothing.

"Maybe they're coordinates?" Emma mused, "Latitude and longitude and..." She scrunched her brow, but a quick search online proved that theory wrong too.

Frustrated, she set the notebook aside and reached for the travel guide. Its dog-eared pages and worn cover hinted at frequent use. Emma flipped through it, searching for any sign of the previous owner - a name inside the cover, highlighted passage, a scribbled note, anything.

"Come on, give me something," she pleaded with the book. But page after page revealed nothing but pristine text. Whoever had used it hadn't circled their hotel, highlighted a restaurant they planned to try, or anything.

Emma tossed the guide onto the bed with a huff. "Well, that was useless."

She picked up the notebook again, her eyes drawn to the numbers. "What are you trying to tell me?"

A yawn caught her by surprise. Emma glanced at the clock and groaned. It was well past midnight.

"Enough of this," she mumbled, stacking the travel guide on top of the notebook and placing them on her nightstand. "It's just a notebook. Not a mystery. And I need sleep."

As she switched off the lamp and settled under the covers, Emma couldn't shake the feeling that she was missing something, even as her logical mind tried to tell her the recipes meant nothing. "Just a notebook," she whispered, but some part of her mind didn't believe it.

Exhaustion soon won out, and she drifted into sleep.

Emma descended the stairs, the aroma of fresh pastries and coffee guiding her to the bakery's small dining area.

Lucia stood behind the counter, her salt-and-pepper curls bouncing in her loose ponytail as she arranged a platter of delicate pastel-colored meringues.

"Good morning, Emma!" Lucia's voice called across the room. "I saved some of our creations for you and Daniel."

Emma's cheeks flushed. "About that, Lucia. I'm sorry I was so distracted yesterday. I had a lot on my mind."

Lucia waved a hand. "Nonsense! You did just fine."

Daniel appeared behind Emma, his hand settling on the small of her back. "Morning, ladies. Something smells amazing."

"Sit, sit!" Lucia gestured to a small table by the window. "I'll bring you breakfast."

As they settled into their chairs, Emma leaned towards Daniel. "I feel terrible. I barely paid attention while Lucia was teaching me."

Daniel squeezed her hand. "Hey, don't beat yourself up. You had a lot on your mind."

Lucia approached, balancing a tray laden with two espresso cups, several flaky pastries, and a small pile of meringues. She set it down with a flourish. "Enjoy!"

Emma picked up a meringue, its crisp shell giving way to a marshmallowy center. "These are perfect, Lucia. I'd love to try making them again when I can focus better."

"Of course!" Lucia beamed. "Now, tell me about your plans for today."

Daniel sipped his espresso. "We were thinking of visiting the Doge's Palace."

"Ah, excellent choice!" Lucia nodded approvingly. "But first, you must try my *sfogliatelle*. It's an old family recipe."

After breakfast, Emma excused herself to brush her teeth and grab her purse. But when she got to her room, she gazed longingly at the leather-bound notebook on the nightstand. The mysterious numbers and recipes tugged at her curiosity, begging to be deciphered. She opened the notebook, hoping something would jump out at her that she'd missed before.

114-11-3, 62-14-10... what did it mean?

Daniel's voice pulled her back to reality. "Ready to hit the streets?" He stood in the doorway, a map of Venice in hand.

Emma hesitated. "I was thinking maybe we could-" She motioned to the notebook.

"Come on, Em. We're in Venice! Let's explore."

She sighed, tucking the notebook into her bag. "Alright, you win."

They wandered through narrow alleys and over arched bridges, the city's ancient charm enveloping them. Daniel's eyes darted from shop to shop.

"I need to find something for Jessie," he said. "I promised I'd bring her something from each place we stayed if she'd man my desk at the police station while we're gone. Any ideas?"

Emma pointed to a display of intricate Venetian masks. "What about one of those?"

Emma followed Daniel into the mask shop, a bell tinkling as they entered. The walls were lined with hundreds of masks, from simple designs to elaborate creations that seemed to come alive.

"Wow," Emma breathed, taking in the kaleidoscope of colors and textures.

Daniel picked up a gold mask adorned with music notes. "What do you think of this one?"

Emma wrinkled her nose. "Jessie's not really the musical type, is she?"

"Good point." He set it down and moved to a mask covered in peacock feathers. "This is pretty flashy."

"Try it on," Emma urged, grinning as Daniel held it up to his face.

"How do I look?"

"Like a bird attacked your head."

Daniel laughed, replacing the mask. "Okay, maybe not that one."

Emma spotted a delicate white mask with silver filigree. "This one's gorgeous."

"It is," Daniel agreed. "But can you picture Jessie wearing it?"

Emma tried to imagine Daniel's no-nonsense sister in the ethereal mask. "Yeah, probably not."

They continued browsing, trying on masks and giggling at their reflections. Daniel donned a red and black jester's mask, complete with bells.

"Now that's a look," Emma teased.

"Perfect for interrogating suspects," Daniel quipped.

As they explored the shop, Daniel's enthusiasm waned. He picked up a simple black domino mask, turning it over in his hands.

"You know, I'm not sure Jessie would ever use any of these."

Emma nodded. "You're right. They're beautiful, but not really her style."

Daniel sighed, replacing the mask. "I thought this would be perfect, but now I'm drawing a blank."

"We'll find something," Emma assured him. "Venice is full of amazing gifts. Maybe we should look for something more practical?"

"Yeah, you're probably right." Daniel cast one last glance at the masks. "They sure are something, though."

They stopped in a shop selling colorful glass figurines. Emma picked up a delicate blue horse. "This is pretty."

Emma watched as Daniel carefully turned a delicate glass dolphin in his hands, his brow furrowed with concern. The shopkeeper, an older man with salt-and-pepper hair, leaned across the counter.

"They're quite sturdy, signore. We package them very carefully for travel."

Daniel set the dolphin down and picked up a miniature Venetian gondola. "I don't know. My sister's not really into knick-knacks."

Emma ran her fingers over a vibrant glass flower. "They are beautiful, though. What do you think about this one?"

Daniel shook his head. "It's nice, but I can't see Jessie displaying it. And I'd be worried about it breaking in my suitcase the whole trip home."

The shopkeeper interjected, "I assure you, sir, we use special packing materials. They survive shipping all over the world!"

"I appreciate that," Daniel said, "but I think we'll keep looking."

Emma nodded in agreement. As they made their way to the door, she caught sight of a small glass cat figurine. It reminded her of Jessie's tabby, but she kept quiet. Daniel was right – these delicate pieces weren't Jessie's style.

Outside the shop, Emma squeezed his hand. "We'll find something. Maybe we're thinking too touristy. What about something she could use at work?"

As they rounded a corner, a familiar voice boomed. "Well, if it isn't my favorite Venetian tourists!"

Bob Thompson stood before them, decked out in a new, even louder Hawaiian shirt, this one covered in pink flamingos. A "Gondolas Are Oar-some!" cap perched atop his head.

Emma couldn't help but smile. "Bob! We keep running into you."

"Venice is smaller than you'd think," Bob chuckled. "Say, have you two tried the gelato at that little place near the Rialto? To die for!"

Daniel said, "Actually, Bob, we're looking for a gift for my sister back home. But we'll keep the gelato in mind. Thanks."

Bob stroked his chin. "A gift for your sister. Well, now. How about—"

"Oh, we didn't mean-" Emma interrupted.

"You don't have to-" Daniel said.

But Bob broke into a huge grin. "Have you seen the masks?"

"Yes, but we don't want anything too touristy," Daniel cut in.

"Or breakable," Emma added.

"Or expensive," Daniel finished.

Bob laughed. "You two don't ask for much, do you? I do have one awesome suggestion. I've found a great shop near San Marcos that sells all sorts of baseball caps!" He pointed to the one on his head. "I can show you the way if you'd like!"

Emma and Daniel glanced at each other, eyebrows raised, trying not to smile, and Daniel shook his head. "That's ok, Bob. I think we'll be ok on our own."

Bob raised a meaty hand in farewell as Emma and Daniel continued up a small bridge.

"Wow," Emma said. "Flamingos in Venice?"

"Maybe it's just his vacation wardrobe," Daniel said with a laugh.

Emma and Daniel strolled through the bustling fish market, their senses overwhelmed by the briny scent and vibrant displays of seafood. Emma's eyes widened at a particularly impressive tuna.

"Now that's a fish," she said, nudging Daniel. "Maybe we should express ship one of these to Jessie. You know how much she loves seafood."

Daniel chuckled. "Right, because nothing says, 'I love you, sis' like a raw fish in the mail."

As they meandered through the stalls, an older man with weathered hands caught Daniel's attention. He stood behind a table laden with an assortment of fish, his eyes crinkling as he greeted them.

"Good morning," Daniel said. "Quite a catch you've got there."

The man nodded. "Been fishing these waters for forty years."

Emma watched as Daniel's eyes lit up with interest. He'd always been fascinated by local trades, and the weathered fisherman seemed to have caught his attention.

"I'm Daniel, by the way. And you are?"

"Leo Russo," the man replied, his voice gravelly but warm. "Been selling fish here longer than I care to admit."

Daniel leaned in, genuinely intrigued. "What's it like, fishing around Venice? Must be quite different from what we're used to back home in the lakes in Minnesota."

Leo's eyes twinkled. "Ah, it's a life, *signore*. We rise before the sun, when the lagoon's still as glass. You got to know the tides, the winds. Each day's a new challenge."

"What kind of fish do you usually catch?" Emma asked.

"Depends on the season. Right now? Lots of sea bass, some bream. Come autumn, we'll be pulling in cuttlefish by the boatload."

Daniel nodded. "And where do you fish? Right in the lagoon?"

Leo shook his head. "Nah, too polluted these days. We go out to the Adriatic. Sometimes as far as Croatia if the fish are being stubborn."

"Sounds like hard work," Emma mused.

"It is, *signorina*. But there's nothing like the feeling of a full net. Or the quiet of the sea at dawn. Makes it all worth it."

Daniel's eyes sparkled as he asked, "Have you noticed any changes over the years? In the fish populations or the water?"

Leo's face grew serious. "Oh, plenty. The water's warmer now, and we're seeing fish that didn't used to come this far north. Some of our old regulars are getting scarce too."

While Daniel chatted with Leo about Venetian fishing techniques, Emma's gaze drifted to the canal beyond. A gondola glided by, its rider's silhouette familiar. Emma's heart quickened. Could it be Valentina?

"*Signorina*?" Leo's voice pulled Emma back. "You look troubled."

Emma blinked, realizing her expression had fallen. "Oh, I'm sorry. It's just... we lost a friend recently. A gondolier."

Leo's face softened. "I'm sorry to hear that. You knew Giuseppe?"

When Emma nodded in surprise, Leo said, "There's been something strange in the air lately."

Daniel perked up. "What do you mean?"

Leo hesitated. "Giuseppe was a friend of yours?"

"Yes," Emma said. "And so is Valentina. Do you know her?"

Leo nodded. "The young girl gondolier. Unusual one, but she's a good person." He shook his head, his gaze on his fish. Then, lowering his voice, he said, "I've noticed some odd goings-on in the canals at night. Always at low tide. Boats where they shouldn't be."

Emma leaned in. "What kind of boats? What were they doing?"

"I'd rather not say more," Leo said with a shake of his head. Then he smiled, and in a louder voice he said, "But listen, if you want a good meal, try Trattoria Al Gazzettino. Best seafood in Venice."

Emma opened her mouth to press further, but Daniel squeezed her hand, a silent reminder to let it go.

"Thanks for the recommendation," Daniel said. "We'll check it out."

As they walked away, Emma whispered, "Daniel, did you hear what he said about-"

"I know," Daniel cut her off gently. "But remember, we're here on vacation. Let's focus on that seafood dinner, okay?"

Emma smiled at him. "Don't worry. I remember we're getting seafood tonight." But as they walked on, her mind raced with questions about Leo's cryptic words and the unusual boat activity. She also thought about the glimpse of the familiar gondolier she'd seen as Daniel and Leo were talking. She would love to talk to Valentina again, if only to hear how she was doing.

Chapter 7

As Emma and Daniel strolled hand in hand through the winding streets of Venice, over foot bridges and alongside canals, the late afternoon sun cast long shadows across the ancient stones. Emma set aside thoughts of Leo's cryptic words and the mysterious notebook and focused on the beauty around them.

They turned a corner and found themselves in a grand piazza. Emma's breath caught in her throat as she took in the magnificent sight before her.

"Daniel, look!" she exclaimed, pointing to an imposing building with a facade of intricate arches and columns.

Daniel squinted at the guidebook in his hand. "That must be the *Biblioteca Nazionale Marciana*," he said. "The book says it's one of the oldest public libraries in Italy."

Emma's eyes lit up. "A library? Can we go inside? Wouldn't Izzy, back home, love to see this?"

As they bought tickets and climbed the steps, Emma stared up at the ornate architecture, wondering how old this amazing building was.

Inside, shelves upon shelves of ancient tomes lined the walls, and the air was thick with the scent of old paper and leather.

"It's beautiful," Emma whispered, her voice filled with awe.

Daniel nodded in agreement. "Look at these manuscripts," he said, gesturing to a display case. He squinted to read the words on the display. "Some of these are over a thousand years old."

"Good heavens." Emma bent to look at the manuscript. "How is that possible?"

As they wandered through the library, Emma found herself drawn to a section on Venetian history. Her eyes glided over the spines of the ancient books as she marveled at the history right here in the room with her.

"Hey, Emma," Daniel called softly from across the room. "Come check this out."

Emma joined him at a large map of Venice spread out on a table. It was intricately detailed, showing not just the canals and streets, but also markings for various historical sites and points of interest.

Emma leaned in to examine the map more closely, trying to find the area they were in, and then to follow the canals to their hotel and the pasticceria. "Incredible," she whispered.

"Look at that," Daniel said, pointing to the gift shop. "They're selling framed quotes by famous Venetians."

Emma took Daniel's hand as they peered at the elegant calligraphy. "That's beautiful. Think Jessie would like one?"

Daniel's face lit up. "Now that's an idea. Let's take a tour first though and check out the gift shop after."

They joined a small tour group led by a petite woman with chestnut hair tied in a loose bun. Her name tag read 'Alessandra'.

"Welcome to the Sansovino Library," Alessandra began, her voice soft but clear. "This remarkable institution began with a donation of several codes by Cardinal Bessarion in 1468."

Emma's heart skipped a beat as her mind swirled from the ancient library back to the leather-bound notebook and odd recipes. *Codes?* Could the strange recipes in the notebook be codes?

As Alessandra led the group through the library's grand halls, Emma tried to force herself to focus on the tour, not wanting to miss any details of this magnificent place. But her mind kept replaying Alessandra's words. "The donation of several codes." How did someone donate codes? Could the codes be used today?

"Here we have the Reading Room," Alessandra said, gesturing to a vast space filled with long wooden tables and ornate lamps. "This room has been the reading place for centuries of scholars poring over our priceless collection."

Emma gazed in wonder at the frescoed ceiling, her eyes tracing the intricate designs.

An elderly gentleman in the group raised his hand. "Excuse me, but I'm a bit confused. Is this the *Biblioteca Nazionale Marciana* or the Sansovino Library? I've heard both names."

Alessandra smiled. "Excellent question. The library is indeed known by both names. It's officially called the Biblioteca Nazionale Marciana, named after St. Mark, the patron saint of Venice. However, it's also referred to as the Sansovino Library after Jacopo Sansovino, the architect who designed this stunning building in the 16th century."

The group nodded in understanding, and Emma found herself impressed by Alessandra's knowledge.

As they moved to the next room, Alessandra stopped in front of a glass case. "This," she said, her voice filled with reverence, "is one of our most prized possessions - the Grimani Breviary. It's a masterpiece of Flemish miniature painting from the early 16th century."

Emma leaned in, marveling at the intricate details of the illuminated manuscript. The vivid colors and delicate gold leaf seemed to glow even after all these centuries.

"And over here," Alessandra continued, leading them to another display, "we have Fra Mauro's map of the world, created in 1450. It's one of the most important examples of medieval cartography."

Emma studied the circular map, fascinated by how people viewed the world nearly 600 years ago. She felt Daniel's hand on her shoulder and turned to see him equally engrossed in the historical treasures surrounding them.

"This is incredible," Emma whispered. "I can't believe we get to see all this!"

Daniel nodded and slipped his arm around her waist. "And I get to see it with you." He planted a kiss on her cheek. "Which makes it even more amazing."

Emma gave him a teasing look as she said, "I can hardly compare to an ancient map of the world." But she couldn't repress a smile.

As the tour ended, Emma hung back, waiting for a chance to speak with Alessandra privately.

"Excuse me," Emma said when the small group dispersed. "You mentioned codes earlier. Someone donated codes to start the library? Can you tell me more about that?"

"Ah, yes, Cardinal Bessarion's donation," Alessandra said, her eyes lighting up. "It was quite remarkable. He gifted the library with over 750 codices in Latin and 250 in Greek."

Emma's brow furrowed. "Codices? I thought you said codes."

Alessandra chuckled softly. "Oh, I see the confusion. Codices is the plural of codex, or codes, which is an ancient manuscript text in book form. These were important historical and literary works."

"Oh," Emma said, still not fully understanding. "So, what kind of... codices did he donate?"

"Well, there were works by Plato, Aristotle, Homer, and many other classical authors," Alessandra explained. "One of the most significant was the Iliad, annotated by the cardinal himself."

Emma's mind whirled. "So, these weren't like... ways to send secret messages, or anything? They were more like codes of conduct?"

Alessandra's laughter echoed softly in the grand room. "Oh I see. I think you're mixing up 'codes' and 'codices' again. While some of the texts might have included moral teachings or laws, they weren't primarily rule books. They were literary and philosophical works, historical accounts, and scientific treatises of the time."

Emma felt her cheeks flush. "I'm sorry, I guess I got a bit carried away with the idea of secret codes."

"No need to apologize," Alessandra said kindly. "It's a common misunderstanding. In fact, the word 'code' *can* mean a set of rules or laws, but that's not what we mean when we talk about codices in a library context."

Emma nodded, grateful for Alessandra's patience. "So, these codices, they were just... regular books?"

"Well, not exactly 'regular' by our standards," Alessandra explained. "They were handwritten manuscripts, often beautifully illuminated. Each one was a work of art in itself, as well as a vessel for knowledge."

Emma smiled, but her shoulders slumped. "Oh, I see."

"You seem disappointed," Alessandra noted.

Emma hesitated, then asked, "Well, I have a notebook I'm confused about." She shook her head, realizing how silly she sounded.

"But it's not nearly as fascinating as the manuscripts you have here." Emma paused, wondering if perhaps, in this vast library, there might be something that could help. "Do you know of any actual Venetian codes or ciphers?"

Alessandra's brow furrowed. "I'm afraid not. Venice has many secrets, but I'm not aware of any specific coding systems. Is your notebook that you mentioned about Venetian codes?"

"Oh. I don't know." Emma said quickly. "It's just something I found." She smiled, hoping she didn't sound too silly.

Daniel appeared at her side, holding a frame. "Found the perfect quote for Jessie. Ready to go?"

Emma nodded, her mind still racing with possibilities about the notebook. As they said goodbye to Alessandra, the woman took Emma's hand.

"I hope you find the answers to your book of codes."

Emma smiled gratefully, "If it is a book of codes, then I do too. Thank you again for the tour, Alessandra. It was wonderful."

As Emma and Daniel made their way towards the library's exit, a distinguished older gentleman approached them, his eyes fixed on the framed quote in Daniel's hands.

"Ah, what an excellent choice," the man said, his voice rich with a cultured Italian accent. "Goldoni's words capture the essence of our beloved Venice, don't you think?"

Daniel nodded, pleased. "Thank you. It's a gift for my sister back home."

Emma's mind was filled with thoughts of codes and ciphers as they exited the library. After a few minutes, she realized the older gentleman had fallen into step beside them. The bright Venetian sunlight momentarily blinded her as they emerged onto the bustling square.

"It appears we are walking the same direction," the older gentleman said. "How are you enjoying Venice?"

Emma glanced at the older gentleman, her mind still buzzing with thoughts of codes and ciphers. She blinked, realizing he'd asked them a question.

"Venice is... magical," she said, her voice tinged with awe. "Every corner seems to hold a new surprise."

Daniel nodded in agreement. "It's unlike anywhere else we've been. The history, the architecture, the canals."

"Ah, yes," the older man smiled, his eyes crinkling at the corners. "Venice has a way of captivating visitors. But tell me, what has been your favorite discovery so far?"

As they turned down a narrow side street, the bustling square fading behind them, Emma found herself wanting to mention the mysterious notebook.

Daniel spoke up. "The food has been incredible. We had *cicchetti* at this tiny *bacaro* yesterday that blew us away."

"Excellent choice," the older man chuckled. "And you, *signorina*? What has captured your imagination?"

Emma hesitated, then decided to take a chance. "Actually, I've been fascinated by the idea of Venetian codes and ciphers. Do you know anything about that?"

The older man's eyebrows rose slightly. "Codes and ciphers? Now that's an intriguing interest. Venice has a long history of secrets and intrigue." He narrowed his eyes slightly as he asked, "Why does this pique your curiosity?"

As they walked, Emma noticed the street narrowing, the buildings pressing closer on either side. Laundry lines crisscrossed overhead, and the sound of their footsteps echoed off the ancient stones.

Daniel shot Emma a questioning look, but she said, "Oh, just a general interest in history and mystery, I suppose. Venice seems like the perfect setting for hidden messages and secret societies."

The older man's eyes twinkled. "Indeed it is, my dear. Indeed it is. Venice has always been a city of masks, both literal and figurative. But tell me, what brought you to our fair city in the first place?"

Emma exchanged a quick glance with Daniel before responding to the older gentleman's question. "Well, we've always dreamed of visiting Europe, and Venice was at the top of our list."

Daniel nodded, adding, "We're from a small town in Minnesota, and this is our first big trip abroad."

"But why did you take your journey now?" the older man asked, his eyes twinkling with curiosity. "If you have always wanted to come, what prompted you to do so at last?"

Emma hesitated for a moment, then decided to share their story. "It's actually quite an interesting tale. Back home, I stumbled upon a mystery that led to the discovery of some buried French jewels."

The older man's eyebrows shot up, and he stopped walking abruptly. "Is this true? Are you a detective, *signorina*?"

Emma laughed softly, shaking her head. "No, not officially. I own a bakery, but I seem to have a knack for solving puzzles."

Daniel chimed in, pride evident in his voice. "Emma's being modest. She not only uncovered the jewels but also helped solve a murder case."

At the mention of murder, the older man's expression grew serious. "I hope you do not encounter any such tragedies here in Venice. Our city has its share of mysteries, but nothing so grave, I trust."

Emma hesitated, thinking of Giuseppe. "We certainly hope not. We're here to enjoy the beauty and history of Venice, not to get involved in any dangerous situations."

The gentleman smiled. "Just so. Allow me to introduce myself. I am Count Alberto Vittorio Casanova."

Emma's eyes widened. "A real count? I didn't know Italy still had royalty."

The count chuckled, his salt-and-pepper hair catching the sunlight. "Ah, not quite, my dear. The 1948 republican constitution ended the legal recognition of nobility titles. However, we still use them as a matter of social courtesy. It's more of a family name now, you see."

As they continued along the narrow Venetian street, Emma found herself captivated by the count's description of old Venice and the history of northern Italy. He exuded an air of old-world charm, and his tailored suit, she noticed, was a stark contrast to the casual attire of the tourists around them.

Their path led them past a quaint shop with delicate lace displayed in the window. The sign above read "Merletti di Serenissima."

Emma's breath caught. "Oh, look at that beautiful lace! Would you mind if I took a quick peek inside?"

Daniel nodded, engrossed in conversation with the count about Venetian history.

As Emma stepped into the shop, the soft tinkle of a bell announced her arrival. The air inside was heavy with the scent of lavender, and all around her, intricate lace creations adorned every surface.

There were several other shoppers admiring the lace creations, and Emma was almost surprised- but not quite- to see Bob at the counter, his flamingo-covered shirt a garish contrast to the tasteful Italian lace. His voice filled the shop as he asked about the price of a lace-trimmed handkerchief. Emma made a mental note to come back later.

Ducking out of the shop, she was just in time to hear the count thank Daniel for a great walk home.

"Home? Do you live nearby?" Emma asked.

Count Casanova motioned them to follow him around a corner where they found themselves back on the Grand Canal. Nearby, a majestic building with a pink and cream facade stood, reflecting the sunlight.

"This is my home," the count said. "The Palazzo Casanova. Perhaps if you are in Venice longer, you can visit me there."

"Oh, it's beautiful," Emma breathed. "But we couldn't impose."

"Nonsense," the count said. "You are welcome any time."

Emma and Daniel said good-bye and the count walked slowly up the street to his incredible home.

"A real count," Emma said. "I feel like now I've seen everything!"

As they rounded a corner, Emma spotted a familiar figure ahead. "Daniel, look. Isn't that Valentina?"

The young woman wore jeans and a stylish top, a far cry from her usual gondolier uniform. Her shoulders were slumped, and she walked with her head down. But it was definitely her.

"Valentina!" Emma called out.

Valentina's head snapped up, her eyes widening as she recognized them. She managed a weak smile as they approached.

"Emma, Daniel. How are you?"

Emma noticed the redness around Valentina's eyes. "We're fine, but how are you holding up?"

Valentina's lower lip trembled. "Not great. I can't stop thinking about Giuseppe."

Daniel squeezed Emma's hand and stepped back, giving the women some space to talk.

"I'm so sorry," Emma said softly as she hugged Valentina. "Is there anything we can do?"

Valentina shook her head. "No, I... I just can't believe he's gone. I'm coming back here to visit the last place I spoke to him..."

Emma's heart sank. "Oh, Valentina. I'm so sorry."

"I've taken some time off work, but..." Valentina trailed off, her gaze distant.

"But it's hard," Emma said gently.

Valentina nodded and sighed. "My heart hurts. And they're pressuring me to come back to work already. I don't know if I can face it yet."

Emma frowned. "Who's pressuring you? Your family? Or is it Marco?"

"No." Valentina's eyes widened, and she took a step back. "No. Please forget I said that. No one is pressuring me." She glanced around as if terrified someone might have overheard her comment. "I shouldn't have said anything. I really need to go."

"Wait, Valentina-"

But the young woman was already hurrying away. Emma followed a few steps, but Valentina was too quick. She soon left Emma standing bewildered on the street.

Daniel caught up to her and took her hand. "Everything okay?"

Emma shook her head. "Something's really not right here, Daniel."

That night after a delicious pasta dinner and a generous helping of gelato, Emma closed the door to her room and flopped on her bed, her mind whirling with the library, Leo, codes, the count, and Valentina. Something was very wrong, and Emma was concerned that Valentina might be in danger. But what could she do to help? Emma was just a tourist here on vacation. If there was something amiss in the gondolier world of Venice, it was certainly not anything she could fix.

She thought about Alessandra's words, and codes. Flipping open the leather-bound notebook, Emma looked at the strings of numbers written along the bottom of the pages. Most of them were three numbers long. 16-3-4 was the first one. They certainly looked like a code, and she wondered how that hadn't occurred to her earlier.

She rolled onto her side and pulled out her phone. Propping herself up with pillows, she opened a search engine.

"Okay, let's see... 'codes with three numbers'," she muttered, typing quickly.

The results flooded her screen. Emma scrolled through, clicking on various links.

"Binary code... no. Morse code... definitely not. Hmm, what's this?" She clicked a link. "'Caesar cipher'?"

But after a quick skim, shook her head. "Nope, not it either."

Emma's brow furrowed as she refined her search. "Maybe... 'three number sets in codes'?"

This time, a promising result caught her eye. "Book cipher? That sounds interesting. Like a library code."

She clicked the link and began reading aloud to herself. "A book cipher is a code in which the key is some aspect of a book or other piece of text. Typically, the book is agreed upon in advance..."

Emma's mind raced as she scrolled down. "Here we go! 'One common approach is to use a set of three numbers to refer to a specific word. The first number represents the page number, the second the line on that page, and the third the word position in that line.'"

She grabbed the leather-bound notebook from her nightstand and flipped it open. "That's exactly what these look like! Three numbers, dash, three numbers."

Excitement bubbled up inside her as she continued reading. But as she reached the end of the article, her shoulders slumped.

"Oh no," Emma groaned. "To decode it, you need to know which book they're using as the key." She flopped back onto her pillows, her mind seeing the thousands of books and manuscripts in the ancient library, not to mention the millions of books in print currently. "And I have no idea what book that could be."

Emma tossed the notebook aside and rubbed her temples. "This is getting me nowhere." She checked the time on her phone and sighed. "I should probably get some sleep anyway."

Reluctantly, she set her phone on the nightstand, on top of the travel guide and notebook.

And then she stopped.

She stared at the travel guide. "Could it be?" she whispered, staring at the small book that had been in the mistaken shopping bag with the leather-bound notebook. "Could the key be sitting right here?"

She pulled the travel guide and notebook onto her lap and looked at the first string of numbers, handwritten at the bottom of the page.

16-3-4.

She opened the travel guide to page 16, ran her finger down the page counting down to the 3rd line, and then over to the 4th word.

If.

She jotted that down above the numbers. The next set of numbers was 45-20-7. She turned to page 45, counted down to line 20, and over to the 7th word.

You.

the next set of numbers, 124-17-10, led to the word "*are.*"

"If you are..."

Emma's heart was beating quickly, and a smile began to spread across her face. She was doing it! She took a steading breath as she looked at the next set of numbers.

But this one stopped her. Rather than a series of three numbers like the others, this one contained four numbers.

98-5-3-2.

Emma thought for a moment. *Page, Line, Word...* could it be...
Letter?

She turned to page 98, counted down to line 5, and across to word
3. The word was "Venice."

"If you are Venice?" she whispered. "That doesn't make sense."

She looked again at the string of numbers. 98-5-3-2. What if 2
meant the second letter?

She jotted it down in the notebook. "If you are e."

The next set also contained four numbers. 156-13-10-1. The word
was "mask." The number 1, if Emma was correct, would mean the first
letter of "mask." *M*.

The next string of numbers, also four digits long, led her to another
letter M. And the next string, the last set of four before the sets returned to groups of three numbers, led her to the letter A.

Emma dropped her pen and fell back against the headboard, staring
at the notebook.

The message she had decoded so far read, "If you are Emma..."

Chapter 8

E mma stared into her cappuccino, dark circles under her eyes. She pushed her *cornetto* around the plate, barely nibbling at the flaky pastry.

Daniel paused mid-bite, his fork laden with frittata. "You okay? Not getting sick again, are you?"

Emma shook her head. "No, I'm fine. Just... tired."

"Tired?" Daniel raised an eyebrow. "You look like you haven't slept at all."

Emma leaned in, lowering her voice. "I figured it out."

But before she could explain what '*it*' was, Daniel's phone vibrated on the table beside him. He turned it over and his eyebrows went up.

"A text from the chief at work, back home, asking me to check my email. Just a minute."

He ate the bite off his fork, set the fork down, and accessed his email on his phone.

As he scrolled, Emma slumped in her chair. She felt an odd mixture of exhaustion and nervous energy that was very uncomfortable. It made her feel like she might never sleep again and like she might fall over asleep at any moment. She took a sip of her cappuccino hoping it might help.

A dark-haired man with a small beard walked into the pasticceria and nodded to Emma before walking to the counter to order.

Emma stiffened. The nervous energy sent tingles through her. Was this man connected to the message in the notebook? Whoever it was, they could be anyone. Her eyes scanned the small shop looking for anyone paying her any undue attention as her mind whirled, trying to make sense of what she'd decoded.

Suddenly, she realized Daniel had been reading his email for a very long time. She looked back at him.

He was staring at his phone as if confused.

"Is everything ok?"

But Daniel didn't seem to hear her. He kept staring at his phone.

Emma bumped his elbow, and he looked up, his eyes wide. "What is it?" she asked.

"I just got a job offer. It's a promotion."

"Oh my gosh!" Emma jumped out of her chair and threw her arms around his neck. "You're getting the police chief position? I knew they would offer it to you! It was that last inspection, wasn't it? You blew them away!"

Daniel untangled her arms from his neck and gave her a half-smile, shaking his head. "Um, no. Not the police chief. It's a big pay raise, but..." He hesitated.

Emma was still grinning. "But what?"

"But it's in St. Paul. I'd have to move to the Twin Cities."

Emma blinked. She dropped back into her chair. "But that would mean leaving Whispering Pines. You'd be hours away. You aren't going to take it. Are you?" Her voice had dropped to a whisper.

Daniel looked down at the frittata on his plate. "I don't know. It's a huge pay raise. I just got the offer, and I haven't had time to think about it." His eyes met hers. "I think... I think..." He shook his head. "I think I don't know what to think. They don't need an answer until next week."

Emma leaned back in her chair. "But do you need to think about it?"

He looked at her, his eyes holding something she couldn't read. "I don't know."

She nodded, as if she understood. Even though she didn't understand at all. If she had an offer to make a ton more money hours away from Daniel, she wouldn't need to think at all. She would have shot off a 'no, thank you' reply before she'd looked up.

She tried not to show the swirl of emotions she was feeling. He was an adult. Of course he could make his own decisions. She needed to respect that. But what did it mean that he even needed to think about it? She blinked quickly, willing her eyes not to get wet with tears. Exhaustion always made her emotions close to the surface. But her blinking was only partially successful.

Daniel wouldn't leave her, would he?

"You were saying something before I got that text," Daniel said. "You figured something out?"

Emma sucked in a breath and let it out slowly. "The notebook."

Daniel's eyes widened as he shoveled another bite into his mouth. "You figured out the recipes? How?"

Emma shook her head, putting thoughts of Daniel leaving her aside the best she could. "Not the recipes. But the numbers at the bottom of the pages. The travel guide was the key." Emma stopped talking and glanced up nervously as a group of tourists entered the pasticceria.

"Emma," he put his hand on hers. "Are you ok? You're acting strange. Is this about the job offer?"

She gripped her coffee cup tightly and shook her head. "I can't talk about it here. Too many people."

Daniel set down his fork. "Okay, now you're really worrying me. What did you find?"

Emma bit her lip. "I was up until four decoding it. It's... it's about me, Daniel."

"About you? What do you mean?"

"I'll show you upstairs. Please, can we go now?"

Daniel looked at his half-finished plate. "But I'm not done-"

"Daniel, please. This is important. You can bring your breakfast with you."

He sighed, wiping his mouth with a napkin and picking up his plate. "Alright, alright. Let's go."

Emma stood up so quickly she nearly knocked over her chair. She took Daniel's arm, pulling him towards the stairs.

"Whoa, slow down," Daniel protested as he grabbed his coffee cup. "The notebook's not going anywhere."

They reached Emma's room, and she shut the door behind them.

"Okay," Daniel said, setting his plate and cup on the small table by the window. "Spill it. What's got you so worked up?"

Emma grabbed the notebook and travel guide. "Look, it's a book cipher. Three numbers - page, line, and word. The travel guide is the key."

Daniel shook his head. "I don't understand."

Emma let out a breath. "Ok. Look." She showed him how the code worked, going slowly, explaining the numbering system.

Then she opened the notebook and showed him the decoded message. Daniel's eyes widened as he read.

"'If you are Emma...' What the hell?"

Emma's hands shook as she held out the notebook. "Keep reading."

Daniel leaned in, squinting at her messy handwriting. "If you are Emma, I think you can help V. If I am gone, she is in danger. G." He looked up, his face pale. "Emma," he stared at her, his mouth hanging open.

Emma turned and paced the small room. "I know. It's crazy, right?"

"Who's V?" Daniel ran a hand through his hair. "Wait, you don't think-"

"Valentina," Emma finished. "It has to be."

Daniel shook his head. "And G... Giuseppe?"

Emma nodded. "Who else could it be?"

"Emma, this is insane. We need to go to the police."

She bit her lip. "With what? A coded message- to me- in a notebook I accidentally took? They'll think we're nuts. I almost think I'm nuts. I can't tell you how many times I've gone over these messages, wondering if I was hallucinating or something."

Daniel stood up and looked out the window overlooking the narrow *calle* below. Tourists were walking by, laughing and talking. A local boy waved to his friends, and they all hurried up the street. But Daniel's focus appeared far away. "Okay, let's think this through. If that's a message from Giuseppe- from a dead guy- how did he get this notebook to you? He's dead."

Emma shook her head. "Not when I picked up the wrong bag at the market. That was the afternoon before he died."

Daniel frowned. "You're right. But that doesn't explain how he would have gotten it to you."

"I have no idea," Emma said. "That's part of why I've been thinking I must be crazy. I picked up the wrong bag. It was an accident."

"And why would he think you could help?" Daniel's brow furrowed. "And help with what?"

Daniel rested his elbows on his knees. "Let's think back. What exactly happened that first day?"

"I wasn't feeling well," Emma said, rubbing her temples. "We met Giuseppe and Valentina in the morning, toured Venice, and went to the Rialto Bridge market in late afternoon where I accidentally picked up the wrong shopping bag."

Daniel's head snapped up. "Wait. What if it wasn't an accident? What if someone switched their bag with yours intentionally?"

Emma shook her head. "I don't think that's possible. How could they have known-" She stopped mid-sentence, her eyes widening. "Giuseppe! Our stop at the Rialto Bridge was his idea! He suggested it, before we left with Valentina! He said we should visit the market at the end of our tour."

Daniel nodded. "Good memory. But how could he have known how to find you, or that you'd have a bag to switch?"

Emma's lips twisted into a wry smile. "Daniel, think about it. He's an experienced gondolier. I'll bet tourists, especially women, almost always buy something at the Rialto market. He would have known that. And he knew Valentina was bringing us. What if he was there waiting when we arrived, and followed us, waiting to switch bags?"

Daniel stood up and ran his hand through his hair. "Okay, so Giuseppe gives us the idea to go to the Rialto Bridge market. He's guessing you'll buy something there- or maybe just that you have bought *something* at some point during the day. So he thinks you'll probably have a shopping bag. And..." Daniel turned to look at her. "And he actually thinks he'll be able to swap bags with you? Doesn't that seem a little far-fetched? This isn't a James Bond movie."

Emma shrugged. "I don't know. Maybe he was desperate. Maybe he had other plans in case I didn't set a shopping bag down. Either way," she motioned to the notebook, "it appears to have worked."

Daniel nodded. "But why us? Why message you?"

Emma flopped on her bed and stared up at the ceiling, thinking. "Remember how interested he was when he found out we'd solved mysteries before? He asked about me being a baker and solving murders. He looked at me so... intently." She looked over at Daniel. "I noticed it a couple of times that morning, actually. Before we left with Valentina. He seemed really interested in my baking and solving murders. If he thought he might be killed..."

Daniel's brow furrowed. "You think he knew he might die? That's pretty morbid. And he sent us a message before his death?"

Emma let out a sigh. "Valentina was trying to tell him not to do something. That it was too dangerous. And the way he looked at me..." She stopped, thinking. "The notebook has recipes," Emma said softly. "Let's assume Giuseppe knew his life was in danger. What if he hoped that *if* he died, we could solve his murder and help Valentina?"

They were both silent for a moment, the weight of this possibility settling over them.

Daniel ran a hand through his hair again. "It's a stretch, Emma. A big one."

"I know." Her voice was barely above a whisper. "But," she motioned to the notebook lying on the small table by the window. "I don't see any other way to understand the messages in that book. And what if we're right? Giuseppe is already dead. What if Valentina really is in danger?"

"Messages, plural? There are more messages?" Daniel said. "Good heavens, Em! What else?"

Emma got off the bed and handed the notebook to Daniel. "Take a look." She pointed to the bottom of each page where she had decoded a date and a time for each recipe.

Daniel flipped through the pages, his brow furrowing. "What's with all these dates and times?"

"I have no idea," Emma said, leaning over his shoulder. "But they're in a different handwriting than the message to me at the front of the notebook. I don't think they were written by Giuseppe, assuming he's the one who wrote the message to me. Each recipe page has a date and time, but I have no idea what they mean."

As Daniel sighed, Emma flipped back through the notebook, scanning the dates. "They're in chronological order from the first of the notebook to the end." As she flipped a page, her eyes locked onto a particular date and her stomach dropped. "Oh Daniel, look."

She pointed to the date at the bottom of the page that had a recipe for 'Stained Glass Sugar Cookies.' "It's the day Giuseppe died."

Daniel took the notebook. After scanning the recipe, which included a variety of minerals that would surely never go into an edible cookie recipe, he turned the page. "And the next date in the book is today."

Emma bit her lip. "We need to talk to Valentina."

She pulled out her phone and started typing a message.

"What are you saying?" Daniel asked, peering over her shoulder.

"I'm asking if we can meet her. We need to tell her about the notebook and these messages from Giuseppe."

Emma hit send, then looked up at Daniel. "Now we wait."

Chapter 9

As they waited for Valentina to reply, Emma laid on her bed and looked out the window.

"You wouldn't really move to the cities. Would you?"

Daniel cleared his throat and stood, walking across the room and straightening a framed painting of a sunrise on a Venetian canal before answering. "I mean, the pay is really good. It could come in useful."

"Useful for what?"

But before he could answer, Emma's phone buzzed. She glanced at the screen and her eyes lit up. "It's Valentina. She's working today."

Daniel nodded. "What'd she say?"

"Just that she's at the usual spot." Emma tapped out a quick reply. "I'm asking if we can book a ride."

With the message sent, Emma said, "So? Useful for what?"

Daniel shrugged. "It's money, Em. It's just... useful."

He paced back to the window, watching people pass by out the window, Emma staring at the notebook, trying not to feel upset about

Daniel considering a job that would take him away from her. When the phone chimed again, Emma let out a breath. "She says 'of course.'"

Daniel nodded, grabbing his sunglasses. "Let's go."

As they headed downstairs, the scent of baking wafted through the air. Lucia stood behind the counter, beaming.

"Ah, going out?" She reached under the glass case. "Here, take some of the nougat cake I made yesterday."

She handed them each a heavy white slice of something that was like a cross between stiff meringue and cake wrapped in wax paper. It contained bits of fresh cherries and halves of hazelnuts. Emma took a bite, and her eyes widened. "Oh my gosh, Lucia. This is amazing."

The flavors danced on her tongue - sweet, nutty, with a hint of honey. "You have to teach me how to make this."

Lucia's face lit up. "Of course! Pick up some of your favorite fruits on your way home. Tomorrow, we make nougat cake."

Emma nodded eagerly. "Deal."

As they stepped out onto the narrow street, Emma took another bite of the cake. "I can't wait to learn how to make this. It's like nothing I've ever tasted before!"

Daniel chuckled. "Always the baker."

Emma playfully elbowed him. "Hey, solving mysteries is hungry work."

As they made their way through the winding alleys, the cake almost distracted Emma from the weight of the notebook lying heavy in her bag and the weight of Daniel's decision that was heavy on her heart.

Emma waved as she and Daniel approached the dock where Valentina waited. The gondola bobbed gently in the water, its sleek black hull gleaming in the sunlight.

"*Ciao!*" Valentina waved, her smile not quite reaching her eyes.

As they climbed aboard, Emma's hand brushed the notebook in her bag.

She glanced at Daniel, who gave her a reassuring nod.

"Where would you like to go today?" Valentina asked.

"We don't have anywhere specific in mind," Emma replied. "Maybe just a lazy trip along the canals? We'd love to see more of Venice's hidden corners."

Valentina nodded, pushing off from the dock with practiced ease. The gondola glided smoothly into the narrow waterway, the gentle lapping of water against stone echoing softly.

"That sounds perfect," Daniel added, his arm draped casually around Emma's shoulders. "We've been doing so much sightseeing, it'll be nice to just... float for a while."

As they drifted past weathered buildings, their reflections rippling in the emerald water, Emma's fingers tightened around the strap of her bag. She knew she needed to broach the subject of Giuseppe and the notebook, but the words stuck in her throat.

"Valentina," she began hesitantly, "how are you holding up?"

The gondolier's shoulders tensed slightly. "I'm... managing. It's been difficult, but I have to keep working, you know?"

Emma nodded sympathetically. "Of course. I can't imagine how hard it must be."

They rounded a bend, emerging into a sun-dappled canal lined with flowering window boxes. The sweet scent of jasmine filled the air.

"This is beautiful," Daniel murmured, his eyes scanning the colorful facades.

Valentina smiled, a hint of genuine warmth returning to her expression. "This is one of my favorite spots. Not many tourists find their way here."

Emma leaned forward, her voice low. "Valentina, there's something we need to talk to you about. It's... it's about Giuseppe."

The gondola wobbled slightly as Valentina's grip on the oar faltered. "What about Giuseppe?"

She took a deep breath. "Do you remember the first day we met?"

Valentina nodded, steadying the gondola. "Of course. Why?"

"I was thinking about the mix-up with the shopping bags at the Rialto Bridge."

"Ah, yes." Valentina's brow furrowed. "That was... that was the last time I spoke to Giuseppe."

Emma's pulse quickened. "At the Rialto Bridge?"

"*Sì*. He was there when I dropped you off, and we spoke while I waited for you two to finish shopping."

Emma and Daniel exchanged a quick glance. She cleared her throat. "Listen, Valentina. Is there somewhere we could talk? Somewhere private?"

Valentina frowned. "We could go to a quiet café?"

Emma shook her head. "No, I mean really private. Where no one else can hear us."

"There's a small park near-"

"Somewhere completely alone," Emma pressed.

Understanding dawned in Valentina's eyes. She hesitated, then said, "The bell tower on San Giorgio Maggiore. It's across from San Marco's. There we can be alone, and we can easily see if anyone's coming."

Emma groaned and Daniel smiled at her. "You asked for someplace private," he said.

"Is that not ok?" Valentina asked.

Emma gave a half smile. "I'm afraid of heights. Even climbing a step stool can make me get vertigo. But it's ok." She nodded. "If we can be alone, let's go."

As Valentina steered the gondola through the canals, Emma tried not to think about being hundreds of feet in the air. She longed to pull out the notebook right now, to show Valentina what they'd discovered. But not yet. Not until they were truly alone.

Emma's heart raced as they climbed the winding stairs of the bell tower. The ancient stone steps echoed with their footsteps, each one bringing them closer to the top.

They emerged onto a small platform. The view of Venice was breathtaking, but Emma barely noticed. Her eyes clenched closed and she gripped Daniel's hand.

"It's ok," he said. "We're alone. And you're safe. There's solid ground under your feet."

"Solid stone hundreds of feet above the ground," Emma corrected him. But she opened her eyes, gulped, and settled herself on one of the benches.

"Okay," she said, turning to Valentina and carefully keeping her eyes from the edge. "We need to show you something."

Hands shaking from the vertigo she was experiencing, Emma pulled the notebook from her bag, holding it out to Valentina. "Do you recognize this?"

Valentina frowned, shaking her head. "No, should I?"

"We think it was Giuseppe's," Daniel said quietly.

Valentina's eyes widened. "What? How did you-"

"We found it," Emma explained. "Or rather, it found us. Look."

She opened the notebook, pointing to the decoded message at the bottom of the first page. Valentina leaned in, her brow furrowed as she read.

"If you are Emma, I think you can help V. If I am gone, she is in danger. G." Valentina's face paled. She stumbled back, her hand gripping the stone wall. "I don't understand. What is this?"

Emma stepped closer, then stopped as she glanced at the city below. "We think Giuseppe left this for us. For me. To help you."

Valentina shook her head violently. "No, no. This can't be real. I need to go." She turned towards the stairs.

"Valentina, wait!" Daniel moved to block her path. "Please, we just want to help."

"You can't help," Valentina hissed. "You don't know what you're getting into."

Emma reached out, gently touching Valentina's arm. "We know you're scared. But we're completely alone up here. No one can hear us. Please, talk to us."

Valentina hesitated, her eyes darting between Emma and Daniel. Finally, she slumped against the wall, sliding down to sit on the floor.

"I don't know what to do," she whispered. "Giuseppe... he wanted to go to the police. But I was too afraid."

Emma knelt beside her. "Afraid of what?"

Valentina looked up, her eyes brimming with tears. "The people he wanted to report. They're powerful. Dangerous. And now he's dead, and I don't know what to do."

Emma watched as Valentina's shoulders shook with silent sobs. She glanced at Daniel, who nodded encouragingly.

"Valentina," Emma said softly, "what's really going on?"

Valentina wiped her eyes, taking a shaky breath. "They... they made us transport packages."

"Who's 'they'?" Daniel asked.

"I don't know," Valentina whispered. "We got text messages. They said if we didn't take the packages, we'd lose our licenses."

Emma frowned. "What kind of packages?"

Valentina shook her head. "Just brown paper wrapped and tied with string."

Emma waited, but Valentina didn't continue, so she prodded. "And what's inside the packages?"

Again Valentina shook her head. "The text messages threatened us not to open the packages. Never to untie the strings or do anything except pick them up and deliver them to the locations they texted us. They said they would be able to tell if we opened them, and it would be stupid to do it. Dangerous."

Emma and Daniel exchanged glances. Valentina's shoulders were slumped. Emma looked around to make sure they were completely alone. No one else was on the observation platform, and when she nodded toward the doorway to the stairs, Daniel checked and shook his head.

"No one," he said. "It's just us."

"Did Giuseppe open one of the packages?" Emma asked quietly.

Valentina's head snapped up, her eyes wide. "No, we-" She stopped, looking away quickly.

Emma caught the lie. "Valentina, please. We can't help if you're not honest with us."

Valentina glanced at the doorway as she said this, and Daniel said, "There's no one there. I just checked."

Valentina let out a breath. "We needed to know what we were doing." Valentina's voice was barely audible. "Giuseppe and I, we needed our jobs. And if we were transporting drugs, then we knew we would eventually be arrested. So we did it. One night, we agreed to open one of the packages."

Daniel leaned forward. "And what was in the package?"

"It was money," Valentina whispered. "So. Much. Money. More than I've ever seen."

Daniel's eyebrows shot up. "When was this?"

"Two days before Giuseppe..." Valentina trailed off, unable to finish.

Emma's mind raced. "And you have no idea where it came from?"

Valentina shook her head vehemently. "No, I swear. But it can't be anything good, right?"

Emma exchanged a look with Daniel.

"Valentina," Emma said carefully, "we want to help. But we need to know everything. Is there anything else you're not telling us?"

Valentina hesitated, then slowly shook her head. "That's all I know. I'm scared, Emma. What if they come after me next?"

Emma reached out, squeezing Valentina's hand. "We won't let that happen. We'll figure this out together."

Emma watched Valentina's eyes dart nervously around the bell tower, her hands trembling as she wrung them together. The young gondolier's fear was palpable, and Emma felt a surge of protectiveness wash over her even as she realized she had forgotten how high up they were as she focused on helping Valentina.

"Valentina," Emma said gently, "is there anyone in Venice you trust? Someone who might be able to help us?"

Valentina shook her head, her dark hair swaying. "I don't know anymore. I thought I could trust Giuseppe, and now..." She trailed off, her voice catching. "I don't even know if I can trust the police. It's likely they are being paid off by someone, and how can I tell which officers I can talk to, and which are involved?"

Daniel stepped closer. "What about Marco? Your boyfriend?"

Valentina's eyes widened, and she shook her head more vigorously. "No, I can't involve him. He doesn't know anything about this, and I want to keep it that way. It's safer for him."

Emma nodded, understanding the desire to protect loved ones. She thought of her own bakery back in Whispering Pines, how she'd want to shield her employees and loved ones from danger.

"What about other gondoliers?" Emma pressed. "Surely there must be someone you can confide in?"

Valentina's laugh was hollow. "That's the problem. I don't know who else might be involved. It could be anyone. The person who sent those text messages... they could be down there," she motioned over the edge of the tower, "watching us right now."

Emma felt a chill run down her spine despite the warm Venetian air. She glanced at Daniel, seeing the same concern mirrored in his eyes.

"Okay," Emma said, taking a deep breath. "For now, we're the only ones you can trust. We'll figure this out together, Valentina. I promise."

Valentina's eyes filled with tears. "Why are you helping me? You barely know me."

Emma smiled softly. "Because it's the right thing to do. And because Giuseppe trusted us enough to leave that message. We turned up, a real detective and, well, an amateur detective, right when you needed us. We won't let his faith in us be in vain."

Daniel nodded in agreement. "We've solved mysteries before, Valentina. We'll get to the bottom of this one too. And as long as no one knows we're anything more than tourists hiring you for sightseeing around Venice, we are safe."

Valentina wiped her eyes, and Emma thought she saw a glimmer of hope breaking through the young woman's fear. "What do we do now?"

Emma leaned forward, her brow furrowed. "Let's start with figuring out who gives you these packages?"

Valentina shook her head. "No one. I get text messages for where to pick them up and drop them off. Sometimes there is a person in the shadows, watching me when I pick up a package or drop it off. Maybe they are there all the time, but I only see them sometimes. I'm sure they are making certain the right person gets the money. But I never speak to them. And they never speak to me. I can't even see if it's a man or a woman. It's always at night. Always in the dark. And they stay in the shadows. I thought I could see their face once, but they were wearing a mask. It was the mask of a cat."

"A cat," Emma echoed. "That's not very helpful"

"Tell me about the text messages." Daniel said. "What number are they from?"

"Always a different number," Valentina said. "But they always begin the same. '*Istruzioni*.' Or 'Instructions.' Then they tell me where to pick up packages and where to drop them off. And then there is always the reminder to tell no one, or I will lose my license or be in danger."

Emma's mind raced. "And after you and Giuseppe found the mo ney..."

"Giuseppe wanted to go to the police," Valentina said, her voice barely above a whisper. "I was terrified."

Emma nodded. "That day we first met. You were arguing with Giuseppe. You were begging him not to do something."

Valentina nodded, a tear slipping down her cheek. "Yes. I was trying to convince him not to go to the authorities."

"You think that's why he was killed?" Daniel asked gently.

Valentina's shoulders slumped. "I'm sure of it. Whoever is behind this must have found out Giuseppe was planning to talk. Or maybe he did talk. I don't know. But either way, they... silenced him."

Emma reached out, squeezing Valentina's hand. "I'm so sorry, Valentina. That must be terrifying."

"It is," Valentina admitted. "It is."

Chapter 10

Emma watched as Valentina's eyes widened, a mix of curiosity and trepidation crossing her face.

"Can I look at the notebook again?" Valentina asked, her voice trembling slightly.

Emma nodded and handed it over. Valentina's fingers traced the coded message from Giuseppe, her brow furrowing as she read it again.

"This is... incredible," Valentina murmured. "Giuseppe left a message for you, Emma. He must have known..." Her voice trailed off, and she swallowed hard. "He must have known he was going to be killed."

Emma felt a chill run down her spine. The realization hit her anew, the weight of Giuseppe's foresight settling heavily on her shoulders.

"How did you get this?" Valentina asked, looking up from the notebook. "The bag, the notebook... how?"

Emma took a deep breath, piecing together the events of that first day in Venice. "Remember how Giuseppe recommended we stop at the Rialto Bridge market after our tour? I wasn't feeling well, but we went anyway. It was so crowded..." She paused, the memory becoming clearer. "He must have switched bags with me in the market. I didn't even notice until we were back in your gondola."

Valentina nodded slowly, her eyes distant. "Yes, that... that makes sense. Giuseppe was always clever. He was very interested in you being detectives. I remember that. He must have hoped you and Daniel would help me if anything happened to him."

The gravity of Giuseppe's actions settled over them. Emma felt a renewed sense of responsibility, knowing that Giuseppe had entrusted them with Valentina's safety in his final days.

Valentina flipped through the pages with trembling hands. Her eyes widened as she scanned the recipes and the decoded dates and times. She came to the graph of wavy lines at the back, glanced at it only briefly, and then flipped back to the recipes.

"Wait," Emma said. "Those graphs on the last page. Do you know what they are?"

Valentina flipped to the back of the notebook. "This? This is a tide chart. Everyone in Venice knows this." She waved it off and flipped back to the recipes again.

"But these dates..." Valentina's voice trailed off. She looked up at Emma, her face pale. "They match. All of them."

"Match what?" Emma leaned closer.

Valentina swallowed hard. "The pick-ups and drop-offs. Every single one."

Daniel frowned. "You mean-"

"This is it," Valentina cut in. "This is their planning notebook. Whoever's behind all this... this is their notebook, where they were organizing everything."

Emma stared. "But how did Giuseppe get it?"

Valentina shook her head. "He must have taken it. From whoever was sending us those texts. Oh good heavens, he knew even more than he told me. That's why-" She choked on the words.

"That's why he was killed," Emma finished softly.

Valentina nodded, her shoulders shaking. "He must have figured out who was behind it all. He was going to expose them."

Daniel ran a hand through his hair. "No wonder they silenced him. He had proof."

Emma's gaze fell on the notebook. "And now we have it."

Valentina looked up, fear etched across her face. "What do we do?"

Emma took a deep breath. "We need to go to the police."

"No!" Valentina's voice echoed in the bell tower. "We can't. That's what Giuseppe did. They'll know. They'll come after us next."

Emma let out a long breath and Daniel nodded.

"Ok," he said. "That's a fair point."

Emma leaned closer to Valentina, her eyes fixed on the notebook. "What about the recipes themselves? They are not real recipes. I think they must also be a code of some kind. Do they mean anything to you?"

Valentina's brow furrowed as she studied the pages. Her finger traced the lines of text, pausing at certain ingredients and instructions. Suddenly, her eyes widened.

"Oh. Wait a minute," she breathed. "You are right. These aren't recipes. They're... locations."

"Locations?" Emma and Daniel echoed in unison.

Valentina nodded, her excitement growing. "Look here, this stained-glass cookie recipe. It's for the date I had a pickup on Murano."

"Where the glassblowers work," Emma said softly. "So, stained glass."

"And where Giuseppe was found," Daniel added, his voice grim.

Valentina flipped to another page. "And this fish recipe? It's for a day and time when I had a drop-off near the Rialto fish market."

Emma leaned in, her heart racing. "What about this one? The *mille feuille*?"

"*Mille feuille* means 'a thousand leaves' in French," Valentina explained. "But in Italian, we say '*mille foglie*' - a thousand pages."

Daniel snapped his fingers. "The library!"

Emma's mind whirled. "So each recipe is a coded location, and the numbers at the bottom are the date and time?"

Valentina nodded, her face pale. "It's all here. Every pickup, every drop-off. Dates, times, locations. For those in the past and the future."

Emma felt a chill run down her spine. They were holding a deadly secret in their hands, one that had already cost Giuseppe his life. And they had figured out what it meant.

"What do we do now?" Daniel asked, his voice low and serious.

Emma's heart raced as she heard footsteps and voices echoing up the stairwell. Valentina stiffened beside her, fear flashing across her face.

"Someone's coming," Daniel whispered, moving swiftly to the top of the stairs.

Emma wrapped a protective arm around Valentina's shoulders, feeling the gondolier tremble. She quickly shoved the notebook into her bag and marveled again that she had been able to forget where they were.

After a moment, Daniel's shoulders relaxed slightly. "It's just tourists," he murmured, stepping back.

As the first heads appeared at the top of the stairs, Emma recognized a familiar face.

Bob emerged onto the platform, his pineapple-covered shirt a strange contrast to the ancient stone walls.

"Well, if it isn't my favorite American duo!" Bob boomed, his voice carrying across the tower top as a group of Chinese tourists entered the tower top behind him. "Fancy meeting you up here!"

Emma forced a smile, dropping her arm from around Valentina. "Hello, Bob." She took a quick glance over the city and looked away before the vertigo hit again. "Quite a view, isn't it?"

Bob nodded enthusiastically, oblivious to the tension in the air. "You bet! Say, did you know that the original bell tower collapsed in 1774? I was just reading about it. Fascinating stuff!"

As Bob rambled on about the tower's history, the Chinese tourists began posing for selfies against the breathtaking backdrop. Emma felt Valentina relax slightly beside her, the gondolier's breathing steadying as the danger she had feared did not appear.

Daniel moved closer to Emma and Valentina, positioning himself between them and the growing crowd of sightseers. His eyes met Emma's, and she gave a small nod. It was time to leave.

Emma stepped off Valentina's gondola onto the weathered stone of the fruit market's dock. The air was thick with the sweet scent of ripe produce and the chatter of vendors hawking their wares.

"This way," Valentina called, leading them through the bustling crowd. "The best berries are at Signora Moretti's stall."

As they walked, Emma turned to Valentina. "I'm making nougat cake with Lucia tomorrow morning. Have you ever tried it?"

Valentina's eyes lit up. "Oh, nougat cake! I haven't had that in years. My *nonna* used to buy it for us children at festivals when I was little. They'd slice it fresh, right there on the spot."

"That sounds wonderful," Emma said. "I'd love to bring you a slice when it's done."

Valentina's smile was genuine for the first time since they'd met at the bell tower. "I'd like that very much."

They reached Signora Moretti's stall, overflowing with vibrant fruits. Emma selected plump strawberries, juicy blackberries, and ripe peaches.

As she held a peach, its fuzzy skin soft against her palm, she sucked in her breath and blinked. "These remind me of the ones I bought that first day here, just before I picked up the wrong bag."

Daniel squeezed her shoulder. "Funny how things work out some-times."

Emma paid for the fruit, and they turned to leave. As they neared the edge of the market, something caught Emma's eye. She blinked, unsure if she was seeing things.

Alessandra, the librarian from the Biblioteca Marciana, was hur-rying down a narrow side street. Under her arm was a brown paper package, exactly like the ones Valentina had described.

Emma's heart raced. Was Alessandra involved in this somehow? She opened her mouth to point it out to Daniel and Valentina but stopped herself. What if she was wrong? What if it was just a coincidence? And she probably shouldn't be calling attention to what she knew about the packages right out in public when she had no idea who was forcing Valentina and others to make deliveries.

"Emma?" Daniel's voice broke through her thoughts. "Everything okay?"

She forced a smile. "Yeah, just thought I saw someone I knew. Must've been mistaken."

As they made their way back to Valentina's gondola, Emma's mind whirled with questions. Was Alessandra carrying the same kind of package Valentina had been forced to deliver? And if so, what did it mean?

Chapter 11

Emma yawned as she tied her apron, the pre-dawn light barely peeking through the pasticceria's windows. Lucia was already at work, measuring out honey into a heavy-bottomed pot.

"Ready to make some nougat cake?" Lucia asked, her eyes twinkling.

Emma nodded, excitement chasing away her fatigue. "Absolutely. What's first?"

"We'll make two cakes today. One with raspberries and blackberries, the other with peaches. Can you start roasting the nuts?"

Emma spread hazelnuts and walnuts on separate roasting pans, sliding them into the wood-fired clay oven. The rich aroma of toasting nuts soon filled the kitchen.

Lucia stirred the honey with a wooden spoon, her movements slow and deliberate. Emma watched, fascinated by the older woman's patience.

"How long do you stir it?" Emma asked.

"Oh, about an hour or so. Until it caramelizes just right."

Emma's eyes widened. "An hour? That's some serious dedication."

Lucia chuckled. "It's worth it for the perfect nougat. Tell me about your bakery back home while you rinse the fruit and keep an eye on the roasting nuts."

As Emma described Northern Pines Bakery, she rotated the nut pans in the oven, rinsed the berries and sliced the peaches. The two women fell into an easy rhythm, chatting as they worked.

"What made you want to open a bakery?" Emma asked.

Lucia's eyes softened with memory. "It was my grandmother's dream. She taught me everything I know. She had always wanted to own her own shop, and when she passed, I knew I had to make it happen."

Emma nodded. "That's beautiful. For me, it was about creating something of my own, you know?"

"I understand completely," Lucia said. "There's something special about building your own business from scratch. Like baking your own loaf of perfect bread, yes?"

They took turns stirring as the honey slowly caramelized. Emma confessed, "I love the early mornings in the bakery. It's so peaceful before the world wakes up."

Lucia nodded. "Ah, yes. It's my favorite time of day. Though som etimes..."

"Sometimes you wish you could sleep in like everyone else?" Emma finished with a grin.

Lucia laughed. "Exactly! But I wouldn't trade it for anything."

"Me neither," Emma agreed, breathing in the mingled scents of honey, fruit, and fire-roasted nuts. "This is worth every early morning."

The kitchen filled with the sweet scent of caramelizing honey.

"Oh, I forgot to mention," Emma said, slicing peaches. "Daniel and I met an actual count the other day! Count Casanova. Isn't that exciting?"

Lucia's hand paused mid-stir, her expression clouding. "Count Casanova? Where did you meet him?"

Emma noticed the sudden shift in Lucia's demeanor. "At the library. He seemed quite charming. Is something wrong?"

Lucia resumed stirring, her eyes fixed on the pot. "No, nothing's wrong. Did you speak with him long?"

"Not too long," Emma replied, studying Lucia's face. "He actually invited us to stop by his home sometime. Isn't that nice of him?"

Lucia's lips tightened. She wouldn't meet Emma's gaze. "I see."

Emma's curiosity piqued. "Lucia, do you know the count personally?"

"It's a small city," Lucia said evasively. "Everyone knows everyone."

"But you seem upset," Emma pressed gently. "Is there something I should know about him?"

Lucia shook her head, her movements becoming brisker. "It's nothing, really. Let's focus on the nougat, shall we? Can you check on the nuts?"

Emma obliged, opening the oven door to rotate the pans. The rich aroma of toasted hazelnuts and walnuts wafted out. "I think they're looking perfect. Shall I take them out?"

Lucia nodded, still not meeting Emma's eyes.

Emma carefully took the nuts from the oven and set them on the counter. "Are you sure there's nothing you want to tell me about Count Casanova?"

Lucia's shoulders tensed. "Emma, please. I'd rather not discuss it. Now, let's talk about how we'll layer the fruit into the nougat. Have you decided which cake you'd like to make first?"

Emma recognized the clear deflection but decided not to push further.

"Alright," Emma conceded. "Let's start with the berry nougat cake. Do we fold the berries in or layer them?"

As they discussed baking techniques, Emma set aside thoughts of the count.

Emma watched as Lucia lifted the pot of caramelized honey from the stove. The thick, golden liquid clung to the wooden spoon, its aroma rich and intoxicating.

"Now comes the tricky part," Lucia said. "We pour this slowly into the egg whites while whisking. It takes a steady hand and patience."

Emma nodded, picking up the whisk. "I'm ready."

Lucia began to pour, a thin stream of honey cascading into the fluffy egg whites. Emma whisked furiously, her arm already aching from the effort.

"Slower," Lucia instructed. "We're not in a race."

Emma eased her pace, focusing on incorporating the honey evenly. "This takes forever," she muttered.

Lucia chuckled. "Ah, you Americans. Always in such a hurry."

"I guess we are," Emma admitted. "Back home, I'm always trying to do ten things at once in the bakery."

"But excellence requires patience, no?" Lucia said, still pouring with unwavering precision. "A good nougat can't be rushed."

Emma nodded, her mind drifting to the mystery of Giuseppe's death and the coded notebook. Would solving this puzzle require the same patience as making Italian nougat? She groaned at the thought, and the ache in her arm, as she continued to whisk.

"How long have you been making nougat?" Emma asked, partly to distract herself from her aching arm.

"Oh, since I was a little girl," Lucia replied. "My *nonna* taught me. She always said, 'Lucia, life is like nougat. You must add the sweetness slowly, and keep stirring.'"

Emma smiled. "Your *nonna* sounds wise."

"She was," Lucia said. "Now, keep whisking. We're almost there."

Emma watched in awe as the mixture transformed before her eyes. The once-liquid honey had merged with the egg whites, creating a thick, glossy mass that clung to the whisk.

"I think we're there," Lucia announced, setting aside the empty pot. "Keep whisking until it loses its shine and becomes soft. Then, we divide and conquer."

They split the fluffy mixture into two mounds. Emma inhaled deeply, savoring the aroma.

"Time for the nuts," Lucia said, handing Emma a bowl of toasted hazelnuts.

As they folded in the nuts, Emma marveled at how the mixture held its shape. "It's like magic," she murmured.

Lucia laughed. "No magic, just science and a lot of elbow grease."

They shaped each mound into a smooth dome, their hands working in tandem. Emma couldn't help but feel a sense of pride as they arranged the fresh fruit on top – plump berries on one, juicy peach slices on the other.

Stepping back, Emma admired their creations. "They're beautiful," she breathed.

Lucia nodded, satisfaction evident in her smile. "Not bad for your first attempt."

Emma's mind raced with possibilities. "You know, I had been thinking of adding this to my bakery's menu back home. But..."

"But?" Lucia prompted.

Emma sighed. "I had no idea it would take this long. We've been at it for hours."

Lucia chuckled. "Ah, there's the American coming out again. Good things take time, Emma."

"I know, but in a busy bakery..." Emma trailed off, shaking her head as she looked around Lucia's bakery and realized what she was saying. "I'm not sure I could justify the time for just one cake."

"Perhaps not for every day," Lucia conceded. "But for special occasions? Your customers would appreciate the effort."

Emma nodded slowly, considering. "You're absolutely right. It could be something for special occasions."

She couldn't help but smile. She'd learned to make macarons in Paris, and now meringues and nougat cake in Venice. Her bakery was going to become quite the international location!

Then she remembered Daniel's job offer in St. Paul and her smile slipped. Why would he even consider it? The thought that he might value a pay raise over being with her stung. And yet, she felt guilty for even thinking that. The last thing she wanted was to be the kind of woman who held Daniel back in life.

As Lucia cut a slice of the fresh nougat cake for her, Emma resolved to talk to Daniel about the job offer today.

Chapter 12

E mma and Daniel stepped off the *vaporetto* onto Murano's sun-drenched quay. The scent of the sea mingled with the smell of melted glass and the faint aroma of nougat and meringue wafting from the box Emma carried. Emma smiled up at seagulls circling in the blue sky overhead.

"I can still hardly believe we're actually in Italy," she whispered to Daniel. "And this is Murano!"

He put his arm around her and gave her waist a squeeze. "And I get to be here with you," he whispered as he planted a kiss on her forehead. "Everything is better with you."

Emma thought about the job in St. Paul but said nothing.

They made their way through narrow streets to Marco's shop, the Fornace della Fenice. As they entered, the blast of heat from the furnaces hit them like a wall.

Marco stood on a raised platform, a group of tourists clustered around him. He held a glowing blob of molten glass on the end of a long metal rod, twirling it with practiced ease.

Valentina stood off to the side, her eyes lighting up as she spotted Emma and Daniel. She hurried over, her voice low. "What are you doing here?"

Emma held out the box. "We brought you some treats. Nougat cake and meringues."

Valentina's face softened. "That's so kind. Thank you."

Daniel glanced around, then leaned in. "We wanted to talk to you about the notebook."

Valentina tensed. "Here?"

Emma shook her head. "Is there somewhere more private?"

Valentina led them to a small office at the back of the shop. Once inside, Emma set the box on the desk and turned to face Valentina.

"We're going to visit the locations mentioned in the notebook," Emma said. "Just to look around, see if we can figure out what's going on with those cash deliveries."

Valentina's eyes widened. "Are you sure that's safe?"

Daniel nodded. "We'll be careful. No one has any reason to suspect we know anything. We're just going to observe, nothing more."

"But what if someone does recognize you?" Valentina wrung her hands. "What if they realize you're investigating?"

Emma placed a reassuring hand on Valentina's arm. "We'll blend in with the tourists. No one will know why we're really there."

Valentina bit her lip, clearly torn. "I don't want you getting hurt because of me."

"We won't," Daniel said firmly. "We've done this kind of thing before. We know how to stay safe."

Emma nodded. "And Giuseppe left me the notebook. He trusted us. Maybe we can figure out who's behind all this."

Valentina sighed, her shoulders slumping. "Okay. But please, be careful. These people... they're dangerous."

"We will," Emma promised. "We'll let you know if we find anything."

Emma watched through the open doorway as Marco's glass blowing demonstration ended. The fiery glow from the furnace illuminated his face, highlighting the intense concentration in his eyes as he shaped the molten glass with practiced precision. With a final flourish, he completed the delicate vase, its curves reminiscent of ocean waves.

The gathered tourists burst into applause, their faces alight with wonder. Marco stepped back from his workbench, a satisfied smile playing on his lips as he wiped the sweat from his brow.

"And that, ladies and gentlemen, concludes our demonstration," he announced, his Italian accent adding a musical lilt to his words. "Please, feel free to browse our shop. Each piece is unique and hand-crafted right here in Murano."

Emma watched as some of the tourists filed out of Marco's studio, their excited chatter fading. Her eyes widened as she caught sight of Alessandra through the doorway, deep in conversation with Marco. What was the librarian doing here?

Before Emma could process this, Alessandra hurried out as well, disappearing down the street.

Most of the crowd filtered into the adjoining shop, their excited chatter filling the air. Emma and Daniel stepped into the shop as well, happy to see Marco's finished creations up close once again.

The shop was a kaleidoscope of color and light. Shelves lined the walls, each one adorned with an array of glass masterpieces. Delicate figurines of animals caught the sunlight streaming through the windows, casting rainbow reflections across the room.

Emma's gaze was drawn to a collection of vases near the center of the shop. Each one was a work of art, with swirling patterns of deep blues and greens that seemed to capture the essence of the Venetian lagoon. A particularly striking piece featured golden flecks that glimmered like stars in a night sky.

Nearby, a group of tourists clustered around a display of large, ornate glass pieces. A chandelier hung from the ceiling, its crystal-clear droplets tinkling softly as a breeze drifted through the open door. Below it stood a magnificent sculpture of intertwining fish, their scales a shimmering mosaic of reds and oranges.

Done cleaning up from the demonstration, Marco strode into the shop, his brow furrowed.

"Everything okay?" Emma asked, motioning him into the office as she held out the box. "Meringue? Or maybe some nougat cake?"

Marco's face brightened. "Nougat cake? I love nougat cake!" He took a slice, but his eyes darted between them. "What's going on? You all look... serious."

Valentina stepped forward, touching Marco's arm. "Nothing to worry about, *amore*. How about lunch? Luigi's café?"

Emma spoke up. "Before you go - was that Alessandra I saw you talking to just a minute ago? The librarian?"

Marco's brow furrowed. "Librarian? I'm not sure who you mean."

"Tall woman, glasses, just left your studio," Emma pressed. "We met her at the library, the Biblioteca Marciana, a few days ago."

Marco shook his head. "Sorry, I don't recall anyone like that. Must have been a tourist who looks like your friend." He gave her an apologetic smile.

Valentina tugged on Marco's arm. "Come on, I'm starving. Let's go eat."

As Valentina led Marco away, Emma turned to Daniel. "Ready to play detective?"

Daniel nodded, a hint of worry in his eyes. "Let's be careful out there."

They left the shop, stepping out into the Venetian sun. Emma's mind raced. Had Alessandra been here? Or was Marco right, and it was a tourist who looked like her?

As they boarded the *vaporetto* back to Venice proper, Emma clutched the notebook in her bag. She was ready to start unraveling this mystery, one location at a time.

Emma leaned against the railing, her eyes fixed on the approaching Venetian skyline. The gentle rocking of the boat did little to calm her thoughts. The woman talking to Marco had looked so much like Alessandra it seemed nearly impossible that it wasn't her. And she'd been talking to Marco after the tourists left. Emma turned to Daniel, who stood beside her.

"I'm certain it was Alessandra in Marco's studio," Emma said quietly. "I'm sure of it."

Daniel shrugged. "Okay, maybe it was."

Emma frowned. "Well, don't you think it's strange? A librarian showing up at a glass blower's studio on Murano?"

"Not really. She could just be interested in glass."

Emma shook her head. "No, I think there's more to it. I didn't mention it at the time, but I saw her carrying a brown package the other day. It looked just like the ones Valentina described."

Daniel sighed. "Emma, brown packages are pretty common. You're reading too much into this."

"No, I'm not," Emma snapped. "When was the last time you saw someone carrying a plain brown package? Most people use reusable bags or those white plastic ones."

"Like the one you picked up by mistake?" Daniel asked with a wink.

Emma nodded, exasperated that he wasn't taking her seriously. "Exactly!"

Daniel reached out to touch her arm. "Hey, what's really bothering you? You seem upset."

Emma pulled away, turning back to the water. "Nothing. I'm fine."

As Venice grew closer, Emma had to admit to herself that she was not fine. Her mind kept drifting to the job offer Daniel had received. St. Paul seemed so far away from their life in Whispering Pines. She felt a knot form in her stomach at the thought of Daniel even considering it.

She groaned. There was nothing she could do about it right now. It was better to focus on things she could do something about.

"We should start with the library," Emma said. "See if Alessandra's there."

Daniel nodded. "Alright, if you think that's best."

Emma didn't respond, her eyes fixed on the approaching city. She knew she should tell Daniel how she felt about the job offer, but the words wouldn't come. Instead, she focused on the beautiful approaching city and the mystery at hand, pushing her personal worries aside.

Chapter 13

E mma and Daniel entered the Biblioteca Nazionale Marciana, the cool air inside a welcome respite from the warm Venetian afternoon. Emma's eyes scanned the ornate interior, searching for any sign of Alessandra.

They wandered through the reading rooms, pretending to browse the shelves. Emma's fingers trailed along the spines of ancient tomes as she kept an eye and ear out for anything related to large amounts of cash, brown packages, or anyone looking suspicious.

"See anything?" Daniel whispered, leaning close.

Emma shook her head. "And no sign of Alessandra either. Maybe we should ask someone?"

They approached the information desk, where an elderly man with thick glasses peered at them over a stack of books.

"Excuse me," Emma said, "we're looking for Alessandra. Is she working today?"

The man smiled and nodded. "She's in the gift shop today. Are you friends? Maybe a visit will cheer her up."

Emma started to ask what the man meant, but a Japanese couple approached the counter asking for help, so Emma and Daniel slipped off to the gift shop.

Emma and Daniel approached the gift shop counter, where Alessandra stood arranging a display of coasters adorned with famous quotes. As they drew closer, Emma noticed the librarian's eyes were rimmed with red, telltale signs of recent tears.

Alessandra looked up, recognition flickering across her face. "Oh, hello! You're the couple from the other day, right?" She forced a smile, but Emma could see the sadness lingering beneath.

"Yes, that's us," Emma replied. "It's so nice to see you again!"

"And you," Alessandra said. "How can I help you today?"

Emma looked over the items in the gift shop, unsure how to broach the subject of Giuseppe's death or the package she'd seen Alessandra carrying. "I'm not sure," she said, trying to think what to say on the topic. "Is there anything you recommend?"

"Well," Alessandra paused her work to consider. "I suppose it depends on what things you want to remember- to bring home with you- from your time in Venice. Have you found something you particularly want to remember? Anything you have especially enjoyed?"

"We've been enjoying nearly everything about Venice," Emma said, "but..." she hesitated, then decided to be direct. "But we were sad to hear about the death of a gondolier recently."

Surprise showed on Alessandra's face. "A gondolier died? That's terrible. I hadn't heard."

Emma relaxed slightly, realizing Alessandra's reaction seemed genuine. Perhaps she wasn't involved after all.

Alessandra's gaze softened as she looked between Emma and Daniel. "But maybe you want to remember happier things, yes? Romantic strolls? It's so nice to see a happy couple. These days, it seems rare for relationships to last."

"Oh, we haven't been together that long," Emma said, glancing at Daniel. "Just over a year, actually. We met while solving a mystery back home."

"How romantic!" Alessandra sighed wistfully. "You must have quite a story."

Emma nodded, then asked, "What about you? Are you married or dating someone?"

Alessandra's smile faltered and she let out a sigh. "I was, until recently. It turns out he wasn't who I thought he was." She blinked and turned away quickly, pretending to straighten some books on a shelf behind her.

"I'm so sorry," Emma said.

Daniel cleared his throat. "Sometimes people surprise us in ways we don't expect."

Alessandra nodded and cleared her throat. "Indeed. But enough about me. Can I help you find anything?"

Emma picked up a set of coasters. "I think I'll take these, actually. They'll make a nice souvenir. And they'll remind us of our time here in the library as well as all the amazing foods we've had here."

As Alessandra rang up the purchase, she said "Enjoy the rest of your stay in Venice." She handed Emma the bag.

"Thank you," Emma replied. "Take care of yourself, Alessandra."

As they left the gift shop, Emma let out a breath and smiled. "I'm really glad she doesn't appear to be involved!"

Emma and Daniel strolled through Campo Santa Margherita, their eyes scanning the bustling olive market. Emma clutched the notebook, her finger marking the page with the martini and margarita recipe.

"See anything unusual?" Daniel asked, his voice low.

Emma shook her head. "Just tourists and locals buying olives. Nothing suspicious here. Although, to be honest, I'm not sure what exactly we're looking for."

"Anything that seems off," Daniel said. "Or anyone who shows up repeatedly in places where we don't expect to see them."

They moved on to Caffè Florian, the aroma of freshly roasted coffee beans filling the air.

Emma flipped open the travel guide as she and Daniel approached the elegant facade of Caffè Florian. Her eyes skimmed the pages, absorbing the information.

"Did you know," she began, her voice tinged with excitement, "that Caffè Florian is the oldest coffee house in Venice? It opened in 1720, which means it's been serving coffee for over 300 years."

Daniel raised an eyebrow, impressed. "That's quite a legacy."

Emma nodded, continuing to read. "It says here that it was a favorite haunt of famous writers and artists. Casanova, Lord Byron, and even Charles Dickens frequented this place."

As they entered the café, Emma's eyes widened at the opulent interior. Gilded mirrors adorned the walls, and frescoed ceilings arched overhead. She lowered her voice, leaning closer to Daniel.

"The guidebook mentions that during the Venetian Carnival, this was one of the few places where women were allowed to enter. Can you imagine the secrets these walls must have heard over the centuries?"

They found a small table near one of the ornate windows overlooking Piazza San Marco. Emma's gaze swept the room, taking in the mix of tourists and well-dressed locals sipping espresso from delicate porcelain cups.

"It's like stepping back in time," she murmured, her fingers tracing the marble tabletop. "The guidebook says they've preserved much of the original décor. Those paintings on the walls? They're from the 18th century."

As a waiter approached their table, Emma couldn't help but share one last tidbit. "Oh, and get this – apparently, Caffè Florian was the birthplace of the Venice Biennale art exhibition. It all started with a conversation right here in 1893."

As they settled themselves at the small table, Emma's eyes widened. There, at the counter, stood Alessandra!

"Daniel, look," Emma whispered, nudging him. "It's Alessandra! Did she follow us?"

They watched as Alessandra paid for her coffee, her eyes redder and puffier than they had been in the shop.

"Does this count as someone showing up where we don't expect them?" Emma whispered.

Daniel didn't answer. He quietly watched Alessandra as she accepted her coffee and turned to leave. Without saying another word to anyone, Alessandra hurried out of the café.

Emma turned to Daniel, her brow furrowed. "That was strange. But I suppose this is a popular coffee shop."

Daniel nodded. "Still, it makes me wonder."

"She was at Marco's studio, and then she's here?" Emma said. Leaning in she whispered, "What if she lied about her boyfriend to explain her tears. What if she's being forced to deliver packages, like Valentina? Or worse, what if she's one of the people behind it all?"

Daniel shook his head and gave her a half smile. "Em, she could be upset about any number of things including her boyfriend. Even the price of coffee." He motioned to the menu. "Which is a valid thing to be upset about here. Look at these prices."

Emma rolled her eyes.

"The fact is," Daniel continues, "we don't know anything for sure. Let's not jump to conclusions."

Emma sighed. "Do you think the cash is connected to the library somehow? Ancient books, rare manuscripts... they could be perfect ways to generate huge amounts of cash."

"That's a pretty big leap," Daniel said as a waiter approached to take their orders. "But I suppose it's possible."

Emma scanned the menu, her eyes widening at the prices. "I think we're paying for the history as much as the coffee here," she murmured.

After a moment's deliberation, Emma ordered a cappuccino, while Daniel opted for an espresso. The waiter nodded and disappeared, returning moments later with their drinks on a silver tray.

Emma wrapped her hands around the warm porcelain cup, inhaling the rich aroma. She took a sip, savoring the velvety foam and perfectly balanced coffee. "It might be expensive, but it's delicious," she admitted.

As they sipped their coffees, Emma's gaze wandered around the café. At a nearby table, an elderly couple pored over a map, their heads close together as they planned their day. A group of fashionable young women chatted animatedly in rapid Italian, their laughter punctuating the gentle hum of conversation.

Through the ornate windows, Emma could see the bustling Piazza San Marco. Tourists milled about, snapping photos of the iconic clock tower and the intricate façade of St. Mark's Basilica. Pigeons strutted across the square, occasionally taking flight in a flurry of wings when a child ran through their midst.

"It's quite a view," Emma remarked, gesturing towards the window. "I can see why this place has been popular for centuries."

Daniel nodded, his eyes on the sparkling water. "It's like watching history unfold right in front of us."

As they finished their coffees, Emma collected her purse and bag, and Daniel smiled at her.

"Have I told you how much I love doing things with you?" he asked, his blue eyes twinkling.

Emma gave him a half smile, her thoughts instantly switching to the job offer. She wished he wouldn't keep saying things that reminded her of it. "You did. Thank you."

As Emma and Daniel strolled into Campo San Giacomo dell'Orio, the ancient square bustling with life, Emma considered Alessandra's comment about her boyfriend not being who she thought he was. She glanced sideways at Daniel. Did she know him as well as she thought she did? What did it mean that he was considering taking a job hundreds of miles away from her? When they had decided to come to Europe together, Emma had taken it as evidence that they would be together long-term. Maybe even get married. But what if it meant something completely different to Daniel?

She looked up at the church's weathered facade that loomed before them, its stones holding stories of centuries past.

"Can you believe this place has been here since 976?" Daniel marveled, his eyes tracing the intricate details of the architecture.

Emma nodded, equally impressed. "It's seen more history than we can imagine. North America wasn't even discovered by Europeans yet when this was built. Some things," she said, "are built to last."

Are we? she wondered.

Daniel nodded. "It's hard to imagine something lasting that long."
Emma sighed.

As they wandered through the square, a familiar figure caught Emma's eye. "Daniel, look. It's Count Casanova."

The count stood near a fruit vendor, examining a ripe peach. Emma hesitated for a moment, then made her way over to him.

"Count Casanova, what a pleasant surprise," she said, offering a warm smile.

The count turned, his eyes lighting up with recognition. "Ah, Ms. Harper, Mr. Lindberg. How delightful to see you again."

"You remember us!" Emma said with surprise. "I wasn't sure you would."

The count smiled. "I don't get to walk home with many Americans. Of course I remember you."

"We were just admiring the church," Daniel said, gesturing to the ancient building.

"Ah yes, a true gem of Venice," the count replied. "Did you know they host a wonderful summer festival here? The aroma of grilled meats fills the air. Children play in the streets. There are live bands. It's quite something. If you are in town for it, you should attend!"

Emma saw an opportunity and seized it. "Speaking of which, Count, we were wondering if we might take you up on your offer to visit your home?"

The count's smile widened. "But of course! In fact, why don't you join me for dinner this evening? I'd be honored to host you both." He held up a peach. "I am hoping my cook will bake peach pastries this evening."

Emma glanced at Daniel, who nodded his agreement. "We'd love to, Count. Thank you."

"Excellent," the count said, clapping his hands together. "Shall we say eight o'clock? I'll have my gondolier pick you up from your hotel."

"Oh, that's all right," Emma said quickly. "We have a friend who is a gondolier, and we're trying to give her as much business as possible."

There was a half-second pause before the count said, "Her?" His eyebrows went up. "We don't have many female gondoliers in Venice." He tipped his head as if hoping Emma would go on to explain.

"Yes, I know," Emma said. "That's part of why I want to support her. Female business owners supporting each other."

As they finalized the details, Emma couldn't help but feel a mix of excitement and apprehension. She had certainly never dined with royalty before! How would she convince her friends and family back home that this was real?

Emma and Daniel strolled hand in hand toward the Bridge of Sighs, its elegant white limestone facade glowing in the late afternoon sun. As they approached, Emma's eyes traced the intricate carvings adorning the enclosed passageway.

"It's beautiful," she murmured, "but so sad when you think about its history."

Daniel nodded. "The last view of Venice for many prisoners."

They paused at the edge of the canal, watching as a gondola glided beneath the bridge. Emma couldn't help but scan the gondolier's face, half-hoping to see Valentina. Instead, an unfamiliar man steered the boat, his passengers snapping photos as they passed.

"I wonder how many secrets this bridge has heard," Emma mused, her mind drifting to the mysterious notebook and its coded messages.

Daniel squeezed her hand. "Probably more than we could imagine. Venice seems full of hidden stories."

They crossed to the other side, finding themselves in a small square bustling with tourists. Street vendors hawked colorful masks and glass trinkets, their voices competing with the chatter of excited visitors.

Emma's gaze was drawn to a nearby gelato stand. "Want to grab a cone? I could use something sweet after all this mystery-solving."

Daniel grinned. "You and your sweet tooth. Sure, why not?"

"What do you think?" Daniel asked, gesturing to the display case as they waited in line. "Stracciatella or pistachio?"

"Stracciatella," Emma replied without hesitation. "When in Rom e... or Venice, I suppose."

As they enjoyed their gelato, a familiar figure caught Emma's eye.

"Oh my gosh. Isn't that Bob? I can't believe how that man gets around," she whispered to Daniel, gesturing towards a man in sunglasses and an "I Love Venice" t-shirt.

Emma tried to duck out of sight, but Bob spotted them and waved enthusiastically. "Well, if it isn't my favorite American tourists! Or are you following me?" He winked, tapping the side of his nose.

Emma chuckled. "I think you're doing the following, Bob. Nice shirt, by the way."

"Thanks! I'm trying to blend in with the locals," Bob said, puffing out his chest. "Swapped out my Hawaiian shirts for this beauty."

Daniel raised an eyebrow. "I'm not sure that's quite achieving the effect you're going for, Bob."

"No? Well, can't win 'em all," Bob shrugged good-naturedly. "Say, Daniel, did you know about the history of this bridge?"

"A little," Daniel replied. "It connects the interrogation rooms to the prison, right?"

Bob nodded eagerly. "Exactly! Prisoners would sigh as they crossed, catching their last glimpse of Venice. But you know what I think?"

"What's that?" Emma asked, curious despite herself.

"This would be the perfect spot for a spy movie!" Bob's eyes lit up as he dropped his sunglasses down and winked at them. "If I was an international spy, I'd do all my secret transactions right here on this bridge. It's got atmosphere, history, and plenty of tourists to blend in with."

Emma tensed slightly at the mention of secret transactions, but Bob didn't seem to notice.

"Well, I'd better be off," Bob said, pointing to a nearby art vendor. "That painting's calling my name. But remember," he added in a stage whisper, "if you two keep popping up everywhere I go, I might have to assume you're spying on me!" With a wink and a wave, he ambled off towards the vendor.

Emma watched Bob's retreating form, his "I Love Venice" t-shirt a beacon among the crowd. She turned to Daniel, her brow furrowed.

"You don't think..." she started, then shook her head. "No, it's ridiculous."

Daniel licked a drip of gelato from his cone. "What's ridiculous?"

"Bob. Being involved in all this." Emma gestured vaguely with her free hand. "The cash deliveries, Giuseppe's death. It's crazy, right?"

Daniel chuckled. "Bob? Our Bob? The guy who just told us he'd make a great international spy?"

Emma couldn't help but laugh. "I know, I know. It's just... he keeps popping up everywhere."

"So do we," Daniel pointed out. "Venice isn't that big, and we're all hitting the tourist spots."

They strolled along the canal, enjoying their gelato in companionable silence for a moment. Emma watched a seagull swoop low over the water, snatching up a scrap of bread.

"You're right," she admitted. "Bob's about as subtle as a foghorn. Can you imagine him trying to coordinate secret cash deliveries?"

Daniel grinned. "He'd probably announce it over a megaphone by accident."

"Or show up to a drop-off wearing a trench coat and fake mustache," Emma added, giggling at the mental image.

"'The name's Thompson. Bob Thompson,'" Daniel said in a poor imitation of James Bond.

Emma doubled over laughing, nearly dropping her gelato. "Stop it! You'll make me choke."

As their laughter subsided, Emma felt a twinge of guilt. "We shouldn't make fun. Bob's actually pretty sweet, in his own way."

Daniel nodded. "He is. Just a guy trying to enjoy his vacation, same as us."

"Same as us," Emma echoed, her smile fading slightly as she remembered the notebook and encoded message from a dead man tucked away in her bag. She took another bite of gelato, savoring the creamy sweetness. "I guess we should follow his example and try to enjoy our vacation too, huh?"

Daniel squeezed her hand. "We will. We'll figure this out, and then we'll have time to just be tourists."

Emma leaned her head on his shoulder as they walked. "Promise?"

"Promise," Daniel replied, kissing the top of her head.

Emma and Daniel strolled hand in hand towards the Rialto Fish Market, the last stop on their list for the day. The scent of the sea grew stronger with each step. As they approached, Emma saw Leo, the old fisherman she and Daniel had spoken with right after Giuseppe's death.

Approaching Leo's stall, Emma suddenly remembered something. She tugged on Daniel's sleeve, her eyes fixed on Leo's weathered face. "Daniel, remember what Leo said about unusual boat activity? He said something about low tides, and there's that tide chart in the notebook. I think we should ask him about it."

They approached the old fisherman's stall. "Leo, it's good to see you again," Emma greeted warmly. The old fisherman's eyes crinkled as he recognized them.

"Ah, the American couple. How are you enjoying Venice?"

Emma watched as Daniel and Leo fell into easy conversation. The old fisherman's eyes lit up as Daniel asked about the man's beloved city and his lifelong profession.

"Venice, she's a fickle mistress," Leo chuckled, his hands busy arranging a display of glistening sardines. "But I wouldn't trade her for anything."

Daniel nodded, clearly fascinated. Emma noticed how Daniel leaned in, genuinely interested in Leo's stories. It was one of the things she loved about him - his ability to connect with people from all walks of life.

"The fishing's changed over the years," Leo continued, gesturing towards the canal. He shrugged, but there was no bitterness in his tone.

Daniel asked about the different types of fish Leo was selling, and Leo launched into an enthusiastic explanation of the local catches.

When there was a pause and no shoppers were nearby, Emma leaned in, lowering her voice. "Leo, when we first met, you mentioned something about strange nighttime activities on the canals. Could you tell us more about that?"

Leo's smile faded, replaced by a cautious expression. He glanced around before answering. "Well..." He paused, weighing his words. "I've been fishing these waters for decades. I know the rhythms of Venice like the back of my hand. Lately, things have been... off."

"Off how?" Daniel pressed gently.

Leo sighed. "It's the boats. They're moving at odd hours, especially during low tide. That's not normal. The canals are treacherous at low tide, even for experienced gondoliers."

Emma's heart raced. This could be the break they needed. "Have you noticed any patterns? Specific times or places?"

Leo scratched his chin, thinking. "Now that you mention it, I've seen more activity around some of the smaller, less-traveled canals. Places tourists don't go. And always when the tide is at its lowest. That's what caught my attention. It makes no sense."

Emma exchanged a meaningful glance with Daniel. It was possible the tide chart in the notebook suddenly made perfect sense.

A policeman walked by, and Leo's eyes darted around nervously. When the officer had passed, Leo said, "I shouldn't have said anything. It's not my business."

"I understand," Emma said. "We think it might be connected to Giuseppe's death."

Leo's shoulders slumped. "That poor boy. He shouldn't have died like that."

"Do you know something about what happened?" Daniel asked gently.

Leo shook his head. "No. No. Not at all. And that's the truth. But if there was any way I could help..."

Emma's heart raced. "You can help. Just tell us about any more specifics on what you've seen? There are a lot of smaller canals in Venice."

Leo sighed, running a hand through his salt-and-pepper hair. "Campo San Boldo."

"Campo San Boldo?" Emma repeated, trying to recall the location from her mental map of Venice.

"It's a quiet spot," Leo explained. "Out of the way. Not somewhere you'd expect to see much traffic."

Emma opened her mouth to ask another question, but a woman approached Leo's stall.

"*Scusi*," she said, gesturing to the fish.

Leo straightened up, slipping back into his role as fishmonger. "I'm sorry, I need to take care of my customers."

Emma nodded, understanding the conversation was over. "Thank you, Leo. You've been very helpful."

As they walked away from the market, Daniel checked his watch. "We should head back to the hotel. We need to change for dinner with the count."

Emma's mind whirled with new information. "Daniel, do you think—"

"Let's talk about it later," he said softly, squeezing her hand. "We don't want to be late for dinner."

Chapter 14

Emma settled into the gondola, her fingers intertwined with Daniel's and the box of nougat cake settled beside her feet. The setting sun painted the sky in vibrant oranges and pinks, reflecting off the canal waters. Valentina stood at the stern, guiding them through the narrow waterways with practiced ease.

"It's beautiful," Emma breathed, taking in the scene.

Daniel nodded, squeezing her hand. "Perfect evening for dinner with a count."

Emma laughed. "Can you imagine what Bridget and Jake will say about this? Dining with royalty? Do you think he eats at a huge table attended by footmen?"

Daniel shook his head, grinning. "I guess we'll find out!"

They glided along, passing under a small bridge, then passing another gondola.

Emma noticed that Valentina was unusually quiet. "Everything okay, Valentina?" Emma asked.

Valentina startled slightly. "Oh, yes. Just... thinking."

"Anything you want to talk about?"

Valentina sighed, her shoulders slumping. "Marco and I... we haven't been seeing eye to eye lately."

"I'm sorry to hear that," Emma said. "Is it about the... situation?"

Valentina shook her head. "No, he doesn't know about that. It's... other things."

Before Emma could press further, the gondola rounded a bend, revealing the majestic Palazzo Casanova. The count stood at the water entrance, a welcoming smile on his face.

"Ah, my American friends!" he called as they approached. "Welcome."

Emma noticed the count's gaze lingering on Valentina as they disembarked. As he offered Emma a hand as she stepped out of the boat, his eyes, slightly narrowed, darted back to Valentina.

"And who is your lovely gondolier?" he asked, his tone smooth as silk. "Has she been your guide for our lovely city as well?"

"This is Valentina," Emma introduced as Valentina handed Emma the box of nougat cake- Emma's gift for the count. "And yes, she's been showing us around Venice."

Count Casanova nodded. "How wonderful." But something in his expression made Emma wonder what he was thinking. Did he find Valentina attractive? He was certainly interested, but, was it her imagination, or did he almost seem almost angry?

Maybe, she thought, he didn't approve of women becoming gondoliers. That was certainly possible.

As Emma and Daniel followed Count Casanova through the grand entrance of Palazzo Casanova, Emma's eyes widened as she took in the opulent interior. The marble floor had an intricate geometric pattern, and a crystal chandelier hung from the vaulted ceiling, casting a warm glow over the space.

"Welcome to my humble abode," the count said with a wave of his hand.

Another man, apparently a servant of some kind, stepped out of a shadowed doorway and bowed to them before walking along the marble hallway and out of sight.

"My assistant, Roberto," the count said when he saw Emma watching the man.

Daniel let out a low whistle. "This is hardly humble, Count."

The count chuckled. "It's been in my family for generations. Allow me to give you a brief tour on our way to the rooftop."

As they walked, Emma noticed the walls adorned with Renaissance paintings and ornate tapestries. The count pointed out various artworks, explaining their historical significance.

"This piece," he said, gesturing to a particularly striking portrait, "is a Titian. One of my ancestors commissioned it."

They passed a set of open doors, Emma peeked inside to see a library with floor-to-ceiling bookshelves. There was actually a ladder to help readers reach the books on the top shelf. She had to resist the urge to pull out her phone and snap photos to share with her friend Izzy, the Whispering Pines librarian back home.

The count led them to a grand staircase with a wrought iron balustrade. As they ascended, Emma's hand glided along the smooth, cool surface as her feet stepped on the worn marble stairs.

"Watch your step," the count warned. "These stairs have seen centuries of use."

Halfway up, they encountered a maid carrying linens. She curtsied quickly and scurried past.

"Ah, that's Giulia," the count explained. "She's been with us for years."

At the top of the stairs, they passed through a corridor lined with family portraits. Emma noticed a resemblance between the count and his ancestors, particularly in the sharp jawline and piercing eyes.

Finally, they emerged onto a rooftop terrace with a breathtaking view of the Grand Canal. A small table was set for dinner, candles flickering in the evening breeze.

"Here we are," the count said, gesturing to the table. "I hope you'll find the view as enchanting as I do."

Emma had to pause and steady herself. Even though she was quite a way from the roof' edge, the height brought back the familiar feeling of vertigo.

"You ok?" Daniel whispered.

She nodded. "I will be."

With a steadying breath, Emma gazed out over Venice, the city's lights beginning to twinkle in the twilight. "It's absolutely magical," she breathed as she took in the sight of the Grand Canal bathed in the soft glow of sunset.

"Please, make yourselves comfortable," the count said, pulling out a chair for Emma, apparently unaware of her fear of heights.

Emma paused and handed the count the box. "This isn't much. But I helped our hostess make nougat cake, and we brought you some, as a small thank you for your kindness in having us here this evening."

The count took the box with a small bow and a smile. "Nougat cake is my favorite. Thank you."

Emma sank gratefully into a chair beside the table and took a steadying breath. She could do this. Already, her heartbeat was slowing back to something close to its normal rhythm.

A waiter appeared with a bottle of wine. The count nodded approvingly. "A local vintage. I think you'll find it quite pleasing. My family is out of the country for the summer, and I've been quite bored here by myself. I miss the entertaining we do when my wife, Francesca, is in town. Thank you for humoring me this evening."

Daniel shook his head. "The pleasure is all ours."

Emma sipped the wine, savoring its rich flavor. "This is delicious," she said.

The count smiled. "I'm glad you enjoy it. Now, enough about my lonely existence. Tell me about your lives back home. What brings you to Venice?"

Daniel cleared his throat. "Well, I'm a detective in our small town in Minnesota. Emma here owns a bakery."

The count's eyebrows shot up. "You own a bakery?" he said to Emma. "So this nougat cake is not just an amateur undertaking. You are a professional!"

Emma shook her head. "I am a complete novice at Italian meringues and nougat. But I am a willing student."

"And you, a detective?" he nodded to Daniel. "How fascinating. So, is that what brings you to Venice? Some international case, perhaps?"

Emma laughed. "Oh no, we're just here on vacation."

The count's eyes narrowed slightly, although he continued to smile. "Of course, that's what you'd say if you were here on an investigation, isn't it?"

Daniel shook his head. "No, really, we're just tourists."

The waiter approached with a silver tray, setting down three small plates in front of them. Emma's eyes widened at the sight of the appetizer. On each plate sat a delicate arrangement of thinly sliced raw fish, artfully draped over a bed of microgreens.

"*Carpaccio di branzino*," the count announced. "Sea bass carpaccio with a citrus vinaigrette."

Emma inhaled deeply, catching the fresh scent of the sea mingled with the bright notes of lemon and herbs. The fish glistened in the candlelight, its pale flesh almost translucent.

Daniel picked up his fork, eyeing the dish with a mix of curiosity and apprehension. Emma knew he preferred his fish cooked, but she admired his willingness to try new things.

She gave him a quick smile before she took a small bite, closing her eyes as the flavors exploded on her tongue. The fish was buttery and tender, melting away with barely any chewing. The vinaigrette added a perfect balance of acidity, while a hint of sea salt enhanced the natural flavors of the *branzino*.

"This is incredible," Emma said, savoring another bite. She noticed a subtle undertone of olive oil and what might have been a touch of fennel. The cook in her wanted to ask for the recipe, but she had no idea if that would be considered rude, so instead, she took another bite.

Daniel took a tentative taste, his eyebrows rising in surprise. "It's actually quite good," he admitted, sounding almost shocked at his own enjoyment.

The count gave a small laugh, clearly pleased with their reactions. "I'm glad you approve. Our fish is caught fresh daily."

Emma took another bite, appreciating how the peppery micro-greens added a pleasant crunch to contrast with the silky texture of the fish. She found herself wondering if she could recreate something similar back at her bakery, perhaps as a savory option to complement her usual sweet offerings.

"So, I am curious," the count said. "I don't know much about how detective work is handled in the States. Are you assigned to a particular region, or state?"

Daniel shook his head and wiped his mouth before answering. "I actually work for the town we live in. It's a small town in Minnesota."

"Ah! That land of ten thousand lakes!" The count's eyes twinkled.

"Have you been there?" Emma asked.

Count Casanova shook his head. "I have not had the pleasure. I'm sorry. But the water appeals to me." He motioned to the Grand Canal. "So, do you ever work with the FBI? Or Interpol?"

"No, nothing like that," Daniel replied. "Just local cases."

The count nodded, seemingly satisfied. "I see. And how did you come to meet your charming gondolier, Valentina?"

Emma explained their first encounter with Valentina and how the hotel and pasticceria owner had recommended her, careful to leave out any mention of Giuseppe.

As the conversation lulled, Emma's gaze fell on a portrait hanging nearby. "Is that Giacomo Casanova?" she asked.

The count's face lit up. "Indeed it is! As a historian of Venice and a descendant of Casanova himself, I'm quite familiar with his exploits."

He launched into a series of anecdotes about Casanova and Venetian history, his eyes sparkling with enthusiasm. Emma listened, fascinated.

The waiter approached with a new tray, this time bearing three steaming plates. As he set them down, Emma's nostrils filled with an intoxicating aroma of herbs and garlic. Before her sat a beautifully presented dish of golden-brown risotto, studded with vibrant green peas and topped with delicate shavings of what looked like white truffles.

"*Risotto al tartufo bianco*," the count announced. "White truffle risotto. A specialty of the region."

Emma's mouth watered at the smells. The risotto gleamed with a rich, creamy sheen, and the aroma of truffles wafted up, earthy and complex. She picked up her fork, scooping up a small bite.

The moment the risotto touched her tongue, Emma's eyes widened in delight. The rice was perfect. The flavors blended Parmesan cheese, white wine, and the unmistakable earthiness of truffles. The peas added a burst of freshness that balanced the richness of the dish.

She glanced at Daniel, curious about his reaction. He was chewing slowly, a look of pleasant surprise on his face.

"This is... wow," Daniel said, his usual eloquence failing him. "I've never tasted anything quite like it."

Emma nodded in agreement, savoring another bite.

"I'm glad you're enjoying it," the count said, a satisfied smile playing on his lips. "The truffles are from Alba, in Piedmont. They're considered some of the finest in the world."

Emma dabbed her lips with her napkin and smiled at the count. "If you'll excuse me for a moment, I need to use the restroom."

"Of course," the count replied. "Down the hall, second door on the left."

Emma made her way through the opulent palazzo, her footsteps echoing on the marble floors. She counted doors, but as she reached for the handle of what she thought was the bathroom, she realized she'd taken a wrong turn.

She found herself in a dimly lit room filled with stacks of boxes and shelves. Curiosity got the better of her, and she stepped inside, squinting in the low light.

"What is all this?" she muttered to herself, running her fingers along a nearby box. It was filled with reams of paper, crisp and clean.

Her gaze fell on several cartons nearby, labeled with the logo of an auto manufacturer. Emma frowned, trying to recall if the count had mentioned anything about his work or how he'd come into his wealth. She was embarrassed that she hadn't asked, and then wondered if it would be rude to ask. She should really have read up a bit more on Italian customs and curtesy.

She peered into the cartons and saw several cans. As she lifted one, she was surprised by its weight. The label indicated it was paint, but not just any paint. As she tilted it in the faint light, she saw the label shimmer with an iridescent quality. Indeed, the label said it was iridescent auto paint.

"Beautiful," she whispered, mesmerized by the shifting colors.

A sound in the hallway made her start and she set the can back in the carton, hoping she wouldn't have to explain what she was doing poking around the count's storage room.

As she stepped back into the hall, she saw the bathroom one door over, the door slightly ajar. With a quick glance up and down the hallway, she shut the storage room door with a click and hurried to the bathroom.

Emma slipped back into her seat at the table, offering a small smile to Daniel and the count. A waiter approached, carrying a tray laden with the third course.

"Ah, perfect timing," the count said, his earlier warmth returning. "This is a local delicacy I think you'll enjoy."

Emma's eyes widened as the waiter set down a steaming plate of pasta before her. The aroma of garlic and anchovies wafted up, making her mouth water instantly. She recognized the dish as *bigoli in salsa*, a Venetian specialty she'd read about but never tried.

The thick, spaghetti-like noodles were a deep golden brown, glistening with olive oil and flecked with specks of parsley. Emma twirled her fork, gathering a small bite. The pasta was perfectly al dente, with a satisfying chewiness. The sauce was rich and savory, with a surprising hint of sweetness from caramelized onions.

Emma found herself torn between wanting to devour the dish quickly and wanting to savor each bite slowly.

Emma hesitated for a moment, then decided to satisfy her curiosity. "Count Casanova, are you in the auto industry?" she asked, setting her fork down.

The count's eyebrows shot up, surprise evident on his face. "What makes you ask that, my dear?"

Emma felt a twinge of guilt for her accidental snooping. "I'm sorry, I took a wrong turn looking for the bathroom and stumbled into what seemed to be a storage room. I couldn't help but notice some beautiful iridescent car paint."

The count's expression cleared, though Emma thought she detected a flicker of something else—concern, perhaps? —before he smiled. "Ah, yes. I do some work with car companies back on the mainland, specifically with Ferrari. We collaborate on designing new paint colors. It's a bit of a passion project."

Daniel's eyes lit up. "Do you really? I love classic cars. How did you get into that?"

Count Casanova pulled his phone out for the first time that evening and glanced at the screen. His eyes still on his phone screen, he said, "Hmm? Oh, yes. Classic cars, quite interesting."

Emma watched as Daniel leaned forward, his interest piqued. "So, Count, how did you get into designing paint colors for cars? That seems like a fascinating niche."

The count's eyes flicked up from his phone, a smooth smile spreading across his face. "Ah, well, it's quite a boring story, actually. But tell me, Daniel, what are some of your favorite classic cars? I'm always curious to hear an American perspective."

Daniel's eyes lit up at the chance to discuss his passion. "Oh, I've always been partial to the '67 Chevy Impala," Daniel said, grinning. "There's just something about that sleek body style and the rumble of the engine."

Count Casanova nodded approvingly. "A fine choice indeed. Of course, here in Italy, we have our own classics. The Ferrari 250 GTO, for instance, is considered by many to be the pinnacle of automotive design."

As the two men delved deeper into a discussion of Italian sports cars, Emma found her attention wandering. She couldn't help wondering if the count was deliberately avoiding talking about his work with car paints, although to be honest, he was probably right. Car paint might be as boring a topic to her as cars in general were. Her eyes drifted to the grand canal visible from the balcony, its waters now dark and mysterious in the fading light.

The count's voice drew her back to the conversation. "Of course, modern Italian cars are engineering marvels in their own right. The Lamborghini Aventador, for instance, is a testament to how far automotive technology has come."

The count's phone buzzed, and brow furrowed as he read something on his screen.

"I do apologize," he said, smiling at both of them. "I've just discovered I have an engagement I must attend this evening. A rather pressing matter. I hope you won't mind if we cut our dinner short?"

Emma and Daniel assured him it was no problem. Count Casanova ushered them towards the door, his smile never faltering, but a clear sense of urgency in his manners.

Emma found herself slightly disoriented as the count led them through a series of ornate rooms, each more lavish than the last. The abrupt end to their evening left her with a nagging sense of unease.

"I do hope you'll forgive the rushed departure," the count said, his voice smooth as silk. "Venice, for all its beauty, can be quite demanding of one's time."

They emerged onto a narrow calle, the stone walls on either side creating a tunnel-like effect. Emma blinked, adjusting to the dim light of the streetlamps. The contrast between the opulent palazzo and the ancient, weathered stones of the alleyway was stark.

Daniel cleared his throat. "Thank you for your hospitality, Count. It was a pleasure."

The count nodded, his eyes darting briefly to the end of the *calle*. "The pleasure was mine. Do enjoy the rest of your stay in Venice."

As the heavy wooden door closed behind them, Emma exchanged a glance with Daniel. The calle was eerily quiet, save for the distant lapping of water against stone and the occasional echo of footsteps from unseen pedestrians.

"Well, that was... interesting," Emma murmured, her voice barely above a whisper.

Daniel nodded, his brow furrowed. "Let's head back to the hotel. I think an evening walk will be perfect after such a delicious meal."

They set off down the narrow street, the cobblestones uneven beneath their feet, their fingers intertwined.

As they walked through the narrow, winding streets of Venice, Emma turned over in her mind the abrupt end to their dinner with the count, Valentina's safety, and the bundles of cash. But beneath it all, a more personal concern nagged at her.

She took a deep breath, gathering her courage. "Daniel," she began, her voice barely above a whisper in the quiet night, "I've been meaning to ask you about that job offer in St. Paul. Have you... have you made a decision yet?"

Daniel's pace slowed, and he turned to face her. In the dim light of the streetlamps, Emma could see something in his eyes that she couldn't read. "I haven't," he said. "It's a big decision, Emma. There's a lot to consider."

Emma nodded, her heart beating faster. "I understand. It's just... I've been thinking about it a lot." She paused, struggling to find the right words. "If you took the job, I... I'd be very lonely in Whispering Pines without you."

The admission hung in the air between them. Emma felt vulnerable, having voiced her fears, but also relieved to have finally said it out loud.

Daniel squeezed her hand gently and then pulled her into a hug. "Emma, I—"

But before he could finish, a group of boisterous tourists rounded the corner, their laughter echoing off the stone walls. The moment was broken, and Emma found herself both frustrated and oddly grateful for the interruption.

As they continued walking, Emma thought about their cozy life back in Whispering Pines. The thought of Daniel leaving, of losing their quiet evenings together, and their less quiet ones with mysteries to solve, made her heart ache.

The longer they walked, the more she wished Daniel would say something, anything, about the job. But he smiled at her as if nothing was wrong, as if he was oblivious to the one thing she wanted to know more than anything. Even more than who killed Giuseppe.

Was Daniel going to leave her?

Chapter 15

B ack in Daniel's hotel room, Emma leaned against the windowsill, her gaze fixed on the dark waters of the canal below. The gentle lapping of water against stone barely penetrated her thoughts.

"What do you think about the count's Ferrari connection?" Daniel asked, breaking the silence and sounding impressed.

Emma shrugged. "It's fine, I guess."

Daniel raised an eyebrow at her tone but didn't comment on it. "So, what's our next move?"

Emma turned to face him. She had to blink a few times to bring everything into focus- the night, the dinner with the count, and even Daniel's room. Her thoughts had been miles away, in Whispering Pines at her bakery, imagining her life there without Daniel if he took the job in St. Paul. "Pardon?"

"What do you think we should do next? About the notebook?"

Emma sighed and crossed her arms. "Right. I think we should go to the next location in the notebook before the scheduled time. We can hang around, pretend to be tourists, and see who delivers the package."

"Really?" Daniel asked, skepticism clear in his voice. "And then what?"

"And then we follow them," Emma said, her tone leaving no room for argument. "If anyone questions us, we'll just act like clueless tourists. Who'd suspect silly American tourists of investigating a murder?"

Daniel shook his head. "Emma, that's too risky. This isn't Whispering Pines. We need to take this to the police. We can show them the notebook and everything we've learned, without any mention of Valentina. That way, she stays safe."

Emma pulled her arms in tighter. "And just hope Valentina is safe, when Giuseppe wasn't? No way. We need more information. We need evidence they can't brush away."

"This isn't like back home," Daniel argued. "We're in a foreign country. We can't just—"

"Can't just what?" Emma snapped, her frustration finally boiling over. "Solve a crime? Help our friend? Is that what you're saying?"

Daniel sighed, running a hand through his hair. "That's not what I meant, and you know it. We need to be careful here."

Emma turned back to the window, her reflection staring back at her from the dark glass. What she really wanted was to confront Daniel about the job in St. Paul, but the words stuck in her throat. So instead, she muttered, "Fine. Whatever you think is best."

The tension in the room was palpable. Emma knew she was being unfair, but the fear of losing Daniel to the cities and all that they held, combined with the stress of the investigation, was wearing on her nerves.

Emma lay in bed, staring out the window at the stars twinkling over Venice. She turned over, pressing her cheek against the cool pillow, and tried to push thoughts of St. Paul from her mind.

"Focus," she whispered to herself. "Giuseppe. Valentina. The notebook."

She closed her eyes, piecing together what she knew. Giuseppe had been killed after threatening to go to the police. Valentina was being forced to transport suspicious packages full of cash. The notebook contained coded messages about drop-off locations and times.

Emma squeezed her eyes shut. "And Giuseppe wanted me to help," she murmured.

She sat up, hugging her knees to her chest. Daniel's caution gnawed at her. But wasn't that why Giuseppe had reached out to her specifically? He was going to the police. Because perhaps he suspected she could do what the police couldn't.

Emma flipped through the leather-bound notebook, her fingers tracing the edges of the pages. The dim light from her bedside lamp cast a warm glow over the cryptic recipes and coded messages. She paused on the page for tonight's date, studying the intricate details of a tiramisu recipe that concealed the true meaning beneath.

Her eyes drifted to the decoded message at the bottom: 23:30, *Calle del Forno*, beside *Stamperia Filippi*.

Emma sighed, glancing at the clock. It was nearly 11 PM. In just half an hour, someone would be making a drop at that old printer's shop across the city. She could picture it clearly - a narrow canal, moonlight glinting off the water, shadows dancing on ancient brick walls.

"If only Daniel had agreed," she muttered, running a hand through her hair.

She understood his caution, but Emma couldn't shake the feeling that they were missing a crucial opportunity. Watching the drop, seeing who was involved - it could provide the evidence they needed to take to the authorities.

Emma turned over and stared at the crack on the ceiling. She imagined following the mysterious figure from the drop point, piecing together another fragment of this dangerous puzzle. But Daniel's words echoed in her mind.

She punched her pillow and turned it over, frustration bubbling up inside her. She knew she should listen to Daniel's experience as a detective. And yet...

Giuseppe had reached out to her specifically. He must have believed she could uncover something the police couldn't - or wouldn't. Emma's fingers tightened around the notebook. She felt the weight of Giuseppe's trust, of Valentina's fear.

"There has to be a way," Emma whispered, her mind racing as she stared at the ceiling. "I can't just sit back and do nothing. And how will I feel if Valentina gets killed because I tried to do what Giuseppe did, and trust the local police?"

She glanced at her phone on the nightstand, considering calling Daniel. Her finger hovered over his name, but she hesitated.

She slid out of bed and padded to the window, looking out over the moonlit streets of Venice. Her reflection in the window stared back at her, and Emma was amazed at the determination she saw etched on her face.

"I can do this," she whispered. "Even without Daniel."

She turned back to her room, stripped off her night shirt and slipped into her jeans and top.

Her bedroom door hardly creaked at all as she slipped into the hall and pulled it shut behind her.

Chapter 16

E mma's heart raced as she slipped out of the pasticceria, the cool
night air brushing against her skin. She glanced back, half-ex-
pecting to see Daniel's disapproving face in her window. But the
building remained dark and silent.

She pulled out her phone, double-checking the location and map.
"Calle del Forno," she muttered, orienting herself. "This way."

Emma set off through the narrow streets, her footsteps echoing off
the ancient stones. Venice at night was a different world - mysterious
and slightly eerie. Shadows danced in doorways, and the lapping of
water in the canals seemed louder without the daytime bustle.

As she crossed a small bridge, a garbage boat chugged by below, its
crew tossing in bags left along the canal's edge.

"Hey!" one of the workers called up to her. "You lost, *signorina*?"

Emma forced a smile. "No, *grazie*. Just... taking a walk."

The man shrugged and returned to his work. Emma hurried on, her
pulse quickening. She turned a corner and nearly tripped over a sleek
black cat that darted out from under a bridge.

"Whoa!" she gasped, steadying herself against a wall. The cat hissed and vanished into the shadows.

Emma took a deep breath, trying to calm her nerves. "Get it together," she whispered to herself. "You can do this."

She rounded another corner, the street narrowing even further. Up ahead, she could make out a faded sign: *Stamperia Filippi*. Emma pressed herself into a doorway, scanning the deserted *calle*.

Emma held her breath, pressing herself deeper into the shadows of the doorway as footsteps echoed off the stones, growing louder. She peered around the corner, her heart pounding.

Three men appeared, their faces obscured by the dim light. They spoke in hushed tones as they glanced around.

One of them hissed something in Italian.

Emma strained to hear any words she knew and wondered how she thought she would discover anything without speaking the language. But still, she inched closer, careful not to make a sound.

Suddenly, another set of footsteps approached, sounding closer than the others. Emma's eyes widened as Marco strode into view, his face tight with anger.

Emma nearly gasped out loud. She swallowed her gasp and shook her head. *He can't be involved*, she thought. It would break Valentina's heart if Marco was involved in Giuseppe's death.

Marco said something loudly as he strode toward the waiting men, his voice angry as he gestured wildly.

The other men turned to him, their voices barely audible. Emma couldn't understand their words, but the tension was clear as Marco jabbed a finger at one of the men, his voice sharp and accusatory. Marco shouted, then took a step back, running a hand through his thick hair.

He turned and Emma pressed herself flat against the door, praying he wouldn't notice her. After a few more heated exchanges, Marco stormed off, leaving the other men glaring after him.

Emma let out a shaky breath, her mind racing. What had she just witnessed? What did Marco have to do with this, if anything? Maybe, she hoped, this wasn't a drop location after all. Maybe she had gotten things horribly wrong, and this time and place had nothing to do with Giuseppe's death, or the packages of cash. And why hadn't she thought to turn on a translating app before she got herself squeezed into a doorway?

A sudden hush fell over the square, and Emma held her breath, thinking the men might have left.

But then she heard the faint sound of oars slicing through water.

She peeked out to see two gondolas gliding up to the edge of the canal. The three men were still on the street, and one of them produced a couple of brown paper packages, seemingly from nowhere, handing them off to the gondoliers.

"*Grazie*," one of the gondoliers murmured, tucking the package beneath his seat.

Without another word, both gondolas slipped away into the darkness.

Emma waited several breaths, counting the seconds, uncertain if the men would leave now or not. And if they did, would they walk this way?

When she'd counted to one hundred, she peeked back out into the square.

It was empty.

Emma's heart raced as she stepped out from her hiding place. She took a deep breath, trying to calm her nerves. Just act natural, she told herself. You're just a tourist out for a late-night stroll.

She'd barely taken two steps when a gruff voice called out behind her.

"*EHI! Ehi, tu!*"

Emma froze for a split second, then broke into a run. Her footsteps echoed off the stone walls as she darted down the narrow *calle*. She took a sharp left, then right, crossing a small bridge. The voice called out again, closer this time.

Panic rising in her throat, Emma ducked down another alleyway. She ran blindly, taking turn after turn until the footsteps faded behind her.

Emma leaned against a shop's doorway and looked behind her.

No one.

She waited, and when several seconds passed and still no one appeared, she let out a breath.

But now, she realized, she had no idea where she was. The twisting passages all looked the same in the dim light. She pulled out her phone and was opening her map when a voice at the end of the passage startled her.

"Lost, Ms. Harper?"

Emma yelped, whirling around to face the speaker. Relief washed over her as she recognized Count Casanova.

"Oh, Count! Thank goodness. I'm afraid I've gotten a bit turned around."

Count Casanova smiled. "It's easy to do in Venice, especially at night. Allow me to escort you back to your hotel."

As they walked, Emma's pulse slowly returned to normal. They passed a small shop that Emma recognized, its windows filled with delicate lace.

"Ah, Sophia's place," the count remarked. "Finest lace in Venice. Did you return the other day? After you stopped in?"

Emma shook her head, amazed again at the count's impeccable memory.

An older woman walked up the street, her back hunched, and paused in the shop's doorway. "Good evening, Count," she said softly.

"*Buona sera*, Sophia," he replied with a nod.

They continued, the count leading Emma through the maze-like streets with ease.

"I was just going to pull up my map," Emma said by way of explanation. "But thank you for walking me back."

"I must warn you, Ms. Harper," he said, his tone serious. "Venice can be dangerous at night, especially in the less traveled areas. It's best to stick to the main tourist routes after dark. And perhaps bring Daniel with you."

Emma nodded, grateful for his concern. "Thank you, Count. I'll be more careful in the future."

As they rounded a corner, the count glanced at Emma. "And what brought you out this evening?"

Emma's mind raced as she tried to come up with a plausible explanation for her late-night wanderings. The count's piercing gaze seemed to see right through her.

"I, uh, needed some allergy medication," she stammered. "My allergies have been acting up, and I thought I'd find an open pharmacy."

The count raised an eyebrow, his expression skeptical. "Ah, I see. But surely you know that the stores are all closed at this hour? Venice is not like American cities, Ms. Harper. Our shopkeepers close up before dinner to spend time with their families."

Emma felt her face flush with embarrassment. Of course, she should have known that. She'd been in Venice long enough to notice the different rhythm of life here.

"Right, of course," she mumbled. "I guess I wasn't thinking clearly."

Count Casanova nodded, but Emma could tell he wasn't entirely convinced. They walked in silence for a few minutes, the only sound the echo of their footsteps on cobblestones.

Before long, they arrived at the door of Pasticceria Ricci. The count gestured towards the entrance with a slight bow.

"Here we are, Ms. Harper. Safe and sound."

Emma thanked him profusely, relief washing over her as she reached for the door handle. It wasn't until she was climbing the stairs to her room that a sudden realization hit her.

She froze mid-step, her hand gripping the banister tightly. How did the count know where she and Daniel were staying? She hadn't mentioned it during their conversation, and she was certain Daniel hadn't either during their dinner at the palazzo.

A chill ran down Emma's spine as she hurried the rest of the way to her room, locking the door behind her. She leaned against it, her heart pounding.

Chapter 17

Emma yawned as she poured herself a cup of coffee in the pasticceria. She couldn't shake the image of Macro striding into the square last night from her mind.

What was he doing with the men who had been forcing Valentina to deliver packages of cash, and who had almost certainly killed Giuseppe?

Daniel skipped down the stairs and came into the restaurant section of the bakery, looking fresh and energetic. "Morning, Emma!"

She forced a smile.

Daniel grabbed a croissant. "Listen, I was thinking we could head over to Murano today."

Emma frowned, her tired brain trying to process this information. "You want to go to Murano?" It seemed so sudden, and after last night, the last person Emma wanted to see this morning was Marco- at least not until she had time to talk to Valentina about what she'd seen.

Daniel looked at her with some concern. "Yes. Murano. I thought you'd be happy to go back. I'd like to pick up one of Marco's glass vases for my office."

"Your office?" No Emma felt even more confused. "Where would you put it? There's barely room for your files as it is."

Daniel shrugged and grabbed a cappuccino. "Oh, you know, I'll find a spot. Maybe clear off a shelf or something."

Emma's eyes narrowed as she studied Daniel's face. A thought struck her, but she held her tongue. Could he be planning for a new office in St. Paul?

"Well, if you really want one, I suppose we could go," Emma said, trying to keep her voice neutral. "Though I'm feeling a little tired."

Daniel's brow furrowed with concern. "Did you sleep okay? We don't have to go if you're not up to it."

Emma waved off his concern. "No, no, it's fine. Just give me another cup of coffee and I'll be good to go."

Emma sipped her coffee, feeling the caffeine slowly start to work its magic. As she and Daniel discussed their plans for the day, Lucia bustled into the pasticceria, her apron already dusted with flour.

"*Buongiorno!*" Lucia called out cheerfully. She paused by their table, her eyes twinkling. "Emma, I was thinking of making a batch of meringues this afternoon. Would you like to join me?"

Emma's face lit up, momentarily forgetting her fatigue and worries. "Oh, I'd love to!" She glanced at Daniel, then back to Lucia and her face fell. "But we're planning to go to Murano. If we're back in time, I'd be happy to help."

Lucia beamed. "*Perfetto!* I'll probably start around three. If you're here, wonderful. If not, no worries."

As Lucia moved away to greet other customers, Emma turned back to Daniel. "That sounds like fun, doesn't it? I've been wanting to perfect my Italian meringues."

Daniel nodded, a slight smile on his face. "It does. And I suspect they are going to be a hit back home."

Emma's smile faltered slightly at the mention of home. She took another sip of coffee and looked out the window at the place where the count had stood last night.

"Well, shall we head out?" she asked, standing up and gathering her things. "If we leave now, we might make it back in time for meringue-making."

As she and Daniel rode the boat to Murano, the memory of last night's encounter kept replaying in her head - Marco arguing with those men, the gondoliers leaving with the packages. She wanted to tell Daniel what she'd seen, but that would mean admitting she'd gone out alone at night. She knew he wouldn't approve.

"You okay?" Daniel asked, noticing her furrowed brow. "You've been quiet since we left."

Emma forced a smile. "Just tired. Didn't sleep well."

They stepped off the *vaporetto* onto the island of Murano and Emma's stomach tightened.

"I'm thinking something in blues and greens," Daniel said. "To remind me of the water here. Will you help me find something?"

Emma nodded and they entered Marco's shop. She glanced up at the sign above the door, Fornace della Fenice, as the bell above the door announced their arrival.

The salesman looked up from behind the counter, his face brightening. "Welcome to Fornace della Fenice. How can I help you?"

"I'm interested in one of your vases," Daniel said. "We're friends of Marco."

"Excellent!" The salesman clapped his hands together. "He has some new pieces. Just finished this month. Let me show you."

As the salesman led Daniel to a display case, Emma wandered the shop, her eyes darting between the delicate glass creations and the door to the furnace room where she could just catch glimpses of Marco's movements as he worked on a glass creation.

"This one caught my eye," Daniel said, pointing to a deep blue vase with swirls of gold.

The man nodded approvingly. "Ah, yes. That's a favorite of mine. The technique is quite challenging. Marco is one of the only glass-blowers in the world who can bring the colors together in such a way."

Emma's gaze landed on a small glass figurine - a gondola with a tiny gondolier. Her throat tightened as she thought of Giuseppe.

"Emma?" Daniel's voice snapped her back to the present. "What do you think of this one?"

She moved closer, examining the vase Daniel had chosen. "It's beautiful," she said, though her mind was elsewhere.

The salesman beamed. "I can wrap it up for you right away."

As he carefully packaged the vase, Emma peeked back into the furnace room. Was it really Marco she had seen last night? Was there a chance she had been mistaken? It had been dark, after all. And she had been stressed, hiding in that doorway, trying not to be seen. Maybe her mind had made her think it was Marco, when it really could have been any Italian man.

"All set," the salesman announced, handing the package to Daniel. "I hope it brings you joy for many years to come."

As Daniel finished paying for the vase, the shop's bell chimed again. Emma turned to see Valentina entering, her gondolier's uniform re-placed by a casual sundress.

"*Ciao*, Antonio!" Valentina called to the salesman, her voice cheerful despite the worry lines around her eyes.

Antonio waved back with a warm smile. "*Buongiorno*, Valentina! *Come stai*?"

Before Valentina could respond, her gaze landed on Emma and Daniel. Her face lit up, the tension in her shoulders visibly easing.

"Emma! Daniel! What a surprise to see you here," Valentina exclaimed, crossing the shop to greet them. She embraced Emma, then Daniel, the genuine warmth in her hugs catching Emma off guard.

Emma couldn't help but notice how Valentina's eyes darted around the shop, as if checking to see who else might be present. When she seemed satisfied they were alone except for Antonio, Valentina's smile grew even wider.

"I'm so glad to run into you," Valentina said, her voice lowered. "I was hoping we could talk more. Are you free for lunch?"

Emma glanced at Daniel, who nodded. "We'd love to," Emma replied, feeling a mix of relief and anxiety at the prospect of discussing recent events with Valentina.

"*Perfetto*!" Valentina clapped her hands together. "I know a lovely little place just down the canal. We can go as soon as I finish here."

Emma nodded, trying to focus on Valentina's excited chatter about lunch plans. But her eyes kept drifting to the workshop door, where she could see Marco's silhouette moving behind the frosted glass.

"So, tell me about dinner with the count!" Valentina's eyes sparkled with curiosity. "I can't believe you were invited to Palazzo Casanova."

Daniel chuckled. "It was quite the experience."

"What was it like inside?" Valentina leaned in, lowering her voice. "I've always wondered."

Emma turned back to Valentina. "It was beautiful. We ate on a balcony overlooking the Grand Canal."

"Really?" Valentina's eyes widened. "What did you eat?"

As Emma described the meal, she found herself relaxing slightly. It felt good to share the experience with someone who appreciated hearing about the details.

"And the count himself?" Valentina pressed. "What was he like?"

Daniel shrugged. "Charming, mostly. Did you know he works with Ferrari? Something with their paint development, I think. It was really a great evening. Though he did seem a bit... off at the end."

Emma nodded, remembering the count's abrupt change in demeanor. She opened her mouth to elaborate, but a movement in the workshop caught her eye. Marco emerged, wiping his hands on a cloth.

He was smiling, but his smile faded as his gaze landed on Emma and Daniel.

"Valentina, can I talk to you for a moment?" His voice was low, tense.

Valentina frowned. "Sure, what's wrong?"

Marco glanced at Emma and Daniel. "Privately."

Emma shifted uncomfortably as Valentina and Marco moved into the furnace room. Their hushed voices carried snippets of conversation through the frosted glass door.

Despite Daniel's look asking what she was doing, Emma stepped closer to listen, but it was no use. They were speaking in rapid Italian.

Emma could see Marco run a hand through his hair, just as she had seen him do last night in the square. He sounded angry, and Emma wished she could understand.

Valentina's voice rose and Emma thought she might have heard her own name.

Marco's voice dropped and Emma couldn't hear him at all, but a moment later the door burst open, and Valentina strode in, her expression stormy.

Emma jumped back, not wanting to be caught listening, but Marco stepped through the door a second later and didn't seem to notice.

Marco scowled at Emma and Daniel. "I would like you to leave. And please, don't come around Valentina anymore."

Emma's jaw dropped. "What?"

Valentina stepped between them. "Marco, stop it. You're being ridiculous."

"I am not ridiculous," Marco insisted. "I am keeping you safe."

"From what?" Valentina demanded.

Marco clenched his jaw as his gaze shifted to Emma and Daniel. "Just trust me."

Valentina shook her head. "No. I'm not going to let you push my friends away for no reason." She grabbed her bag from behind the counter. "Come on, Emma, Daniel. Let's go."

As they left the shop, Emma heard Marco call after them, "Valentina, wait!"

But Valentina didn't look back. She marched down the street, her face flushed with anger.

"I can't believe him," she muttered. "What's gotten into him?"

Emma exchanged a worried glance with Daniel. She wanted to tell Valentina what she'd seen last night, but the words stuck in her throat.

Valentina led the way to a nearby café and Emma followed, her mind racing.

As they settled at a table overlooking the canal, Emma took a deep breath. "I need to tell you both something," she said, her fingers fidgeting with the menu.

Daniel raised an eyebrow.

Emma glanced at Valentina, then back to Daniel. "Last night, I went to one of the locations from the notebook."

Daniel's eyes widened. "You did what?"

Emma held up a hand to stop Daniel's outburst. "I saw Marco there," she continued, her voice low as she leaned toward Valentina. "He was arguing with some men, and then two gondoliers showed up. They were both given packages wrapped in brown paper."

Valentina's face paled. "No, that's impossible. You must be mistaken. Marco cannot be involved. He knows nothing about this."

Emma shook her head. "I hoped I was wrong, but after how he just acted... telling you to stay away from us with no apparent reason? I'm sure it was him."

Daniel leaned back in his chair, his expression hard. "Emma, what were you thinking? Why would you go out alone like that? We talked about it and agreed not to go. It could have been dangerous."

"*You* decided not to go. I never agreed. Just because you decide something doesn't mean I agree with you," Emma shot back. "And I asked you to come with me. But you didn't want to."

"That doesn't mean you should have gone by yourself!"

Valentina held up her hands. "Wait, please. Emma, how can you be absolutely certain it was Marco?"

Emma let out a sigh. "You know the way he runs his hand through his hair when he's upset?"

Valentina nodded, her eyes wide.

"He did that same thing last night, after arguing with the other men there. It was him. His walk, his voice, everything. And what else could explain him asking you not to see us? That's not like him, is it?"

Valentina shook her head. "It's not like him at all. I don't understand what he is doing."

"I'm sorry, Valentina," Emma said quietly. "I wish I wasn't sure. But I am. Somehow, he is involved."

Valentina's eyes filled with tears. "But he can't be... he can't be a part of what happened to Giuseppe. He just can't be!"

"I don't know what part he's playing," Emma said. "But he was definitely there."

Daniel sighed. "This is incredibly dangerous. We need to go to the police with this information."

"No!" Valentina grabbed his arm. "Please, not yet. Let me talk to Marco first. There has to be an explanation."

Daniel opened his mouth to argue, but Valentina cut him off. "And it's not safe for me. If you go, I mean. You don't know how these things work here. Please. If you want us to be safe, promise me you won't go to the police until we have proof." She looked from Daniel to Emma. "More proof than Giuseppe had. I don't want to end up like he did."

Emma glanced at Daniel and saw his worried expression. Then she saw the vase in the package on the table- the vase that wouldn't fit in his office in Whispering Pines.

Marco wasn't the only boyfriend around who was doing things that didn't make sense.

Emma realized she was waiting for Daniel to agree. But if he was already buying decorations for his office in St. Paul and planning to leave her, then why was she waiting for him?

"I promise, Valentina," she said with a hard glance at Daniel. "I promise I'll get proof before I go to the police."

Chapter 18

A man walked past their table on the sidewalk by the canal and entered the café.

Emma's eyes widened as she followed him to the counter. She leaned in close to Daniel and Valentina, her voice barely above a whisper.

"That man ordering coffee! He was there last night, at the drop!"

Daniel tensed, his gaze shifting to the counter inside the café. "Are you sure?"

Emma nodded. "Positive. He was one of the men Marco was arguing with."

Valentina leaned to the side to get a better look. After a moment, she said, "I've never seen him before."

"This is perfect!" Emma said, her mind racing. "We can follow him! See where he goes. And maybe we can figure out who he is!"

Daniel frowned and shook his head. "Emma, this is getting crazy. That could be extremely dangerous."

"Or it could be exactly what we need! It's daylight. There are other people around." She motioned to the tourists and locals along the street. "We can blend in. And if anything happens, we can duck into a shop and disappear." She looked back to the counter where the shopkeeper was handing the man a coffee in a to-go cup. "But we need to decide fast," Emma pressed.

Valentina shook her head. "I can't go. If he's involved, he might recognize me."

Emma turned to Daniel, her eyes pleading. "We have to do something. This could be our chance to figure out what's going on."

Daniel hesitated, then sighed. "Alright. But we're careful, okay? No risks."

"Agreed," Emma said, relief washing over her. She squeezed Valentina's hand. "We'll be in touch soon. Stay safe."

As the man collected his coffee and headed for the door, Emma and Daniel watched from the corners of their eyes, ready to follow as soon as he'd moved a distance from the café. Emma's heart pounded as she collected her purse and glanced up the street.

A line from Sherlock Holmes went through her mind. The game was afoot.

Emma and Daniel strolled as casually as they could along the main street of Murano, their eyes darting between the colorful glass displays and their target. The man walked briskly, his coffee cup in hand, apparently oblivious to their presence.

"Look at that vase," Emma said clearly, pointing to a shop window. "Isn't it beautiful?"

Daniel nodded, playing along. "Absolutely stunning."

But they couldn't pause to examine anything. The man was moving too quickly.

They continued up the street, always keeping the man in sight. As he approached the *vaporetto* stop and glanced at his watch, Emma's heart raced.

"I think he's going to get on," she whispered. "We need to follow."

They stood just outside the small circle of people waiting for the water taxi. The man only glanced back once, and then it was toward the shops, not at Emma or Daniel. Emma felt a small smile on her lips. This was almost fun.

When the *vaporetto* approached, Emma and Daniel boarded the boat last of the group, well after their target had settled himself in one of the plastic seats, careful to keep their distance. The ride to Venice felt endless, Emma's nerves on edge with each passing moment.

They came to the first stop, and the man didn't make any move to get off, so Emma and Daniel stayed put as well. As passengers came and went, Emma shifted to keep a line of sight on their target.

Finally, just before a small stop on a side canal, the man stood. He was the only one getting off here, and Emma wondered how to keep him from noticing them.

"Wait until he's stepped off to get up," Daniel whispered.

Emma nodded.

When the man had disembarked, Emma tugged Daniel's sleeve. "Come on."

They followed him through winding streets, past bustling cafes and quiet residential areas. On a narrow *calle*, where they were the only ones, Emma and Daniel fell back far enough that they lost sight of the man. Hurrying to a corner, they just spotted him up a side street and hurried forward.

They rounded the corner and found themselves in a secluded square with flowers tumbling over a stone wall beside an ancient church that stood at the water's edge.

They stopped, aware that they and the man were the only ones around.

The man approached the canal at the corner of the church, then without glancing back, stepped into the canal and seemed to vanish into thin air.

"What on earth?" Daniel said.

Emma started forward. "We need to see where he went!"

Daniel grabbed her arm. "Hold on. We can't just rush in. Let's walk slowly. As if we just happen to be strolling past."

"But he disappeared!"

"Emma, think about it. If there's some kind of hidden entrance there, who knows what – or who – might be on the other side?"

Emma hesitated, torn between her curiosity and Daniel's logic.

"We'll come back later," Daniel said firmly. "When it's safer. When we haven't just been following him. We can check it out then."

Emma sighed, reluctantly nodding. "You're right. But we are coming back, aren't we?"

"Of course," Daniel assured her. "We just need to be smart about this."

As they turned to leave, Emma cast one last glance at the spot where the man had vanished, her mind buzzing with possibilities.

Emma paced in her hotel room, anxious for Valentina to arrive. When a soft knock came at the door, she rushed to open it.

"Come in, quick," Emma said, ushering Valentina inside.

Daniel sat on the edge of the bed, his brow furrowed. "We're glad you could make it."

Valentina glanced around nervously. She held a plate of meringues in her hand. "The shop owner gave me these when I said I was here to see you." She held out the plate to Emma. "But I am too nervous to eat. Tell me, what did you find?"

Emma took the plate of meringues and bit into one absent-mindedly as she sat beside Daniel.

Valentina waited. "Well?"

Daniel leaned forward. "He led us to an old church by a canal. Then he just... vanished."

"Vanished?" Valentina stared.

Emma nodded. "It was like he stepped right into the water and disappeared."

Valentina bit her lip, thinking. "Maybe... maybe there's something we can't see from land. I could take you in my gondola."

"Are you sure?" Emma asked. "We don't want to get you in trouble."

Valentina squared her shoulders. "Marco is not in charge of me. He should know that. and I need to know what's going on. Let's go."

Daniel grabbed a meringue and the three of them slipped out of the hotel and made their way to Valentina's gondola. As they glided through the canals, Emma watched for the ancient church.

"There it is," Daniel said, pointing to flowers tumbling over a stone wall.

Valentina steered the gondola closer, but as they approached, Emma's excitement turned to disappointment. The church wall disappeared into the water, just as it looked like it did from the square, with no sign of an entrance.

"I don't understand," Emma said. "He went right here."

Valentina slowed her gondola and studied the wall. "The tide is high right now. There might be an opening underneath, only visible at low tide. There are some places like that in Venice."

Emma's eyes lit up. "The notebook! There was a tide chart in the back. That must be why!"

Daniel nodded. "That makes sense! When we were here, where was the tide?"

Emma shrugged, but Valentina looked thoughtful. "It was how long... maybe an hour after you left the café?" When Daniel nodded, she said, "Yes, it would have been low tide then."

"We need to come back when the tide is low," Emma said, a smile spreading across her face.

As they turned the gondola around, Valentina said, "All right. We'll look at the tide chart and find a time to return."

Emma watched as Valentina maneuvered the gondola up to the small dock behind Pasticceria Ricci. As Emma and Daniel climbed out, Valentina's phone chimed.

Valentina glanced at the screen and scowled. "It's Marco. I told him I don't want to talk to him."

She shoved the phone back in her pocket without reading the message.

Daniel paused, one foot on the dock. "Maybe you should read it," he said gently. "There might be some misunderstanding about what Emma saw."

Valentina shook her head. "No. I'm tired of him trying to control me."

"I get that," Daniel said. "But maybe hear him out?"

Valentina sighed and pulled out her phone. As she read the message, she dropped onto the seat in her gondola and her face drained of color.

"What is it?" Emma asked.

Valentina's hand shook as she held out the phone. "It's... it's not from Marco. Someone has his phone."

Daniel took the phone and read aloud: "We have Marco. Don't call police. Go home and wait for instructions."

Emma's heart raced. "Oh my gosh, Valentina, I am so sorry. This is insane. What are we going to do?"

Valentina's eyes filled with tears. "What if they hurt him?"

Daniel bent and put a hand on Valentina's shoulder. "We'll figure this out. Let's go inside and talk."

"No," Valentina shook her head. "They said to go home and wait. Maybe they know where I am right now!" She looked up and down the deserted canal, panic clear in her expression.

"I don't think they could be," said Emma.

But Valentina stood and picked up her oar. "I'm going home. Oh, what have I done?"

Chapter 19

Emma jolted awake to the sound of her phone ringing. She fumbled for it, her heart racing as she saw Valentina's name on the screen.

"Valentina? What's wrong?"

"Emma, I just got home, and I found a ransom note in my door jamb!" Valentina's voice shook as if she was on the verge of hysterics. "They want me to bring you and Daniel to a fishing boat outside Venice at midnight on Saturday!"

Emma sat up, fully alert now. "What?"

Valentina repeated what the ransom note said.

Emma tried to understand. "Daniel and I are what they want as ransom for releasing Marco?" She paused as the full weight of the situation sank in. "But you won't do that, will you? You're telling me this, Valentina. So, you're not planning to do it... right?"

"No, Emma, of course not! But when I don't bring you to them on Saturday night..." Valentina's voice broke into a choking sob. "They'll kill Marco!"

Emma stood and paced across her room. She glanced at the clock on the nightstand. It read 1:15 AM. "It's Friday. So tomorrow night." She turned and paced the other way. "We need to talk to Daniel. But he's asleep. It's the middle of the night. Is it safe for us to meet right now, in the dark?"

On the other end of the line, Emma heard Valentina sob.

Emma paced to the window and stared out into the deserted street. She remembered her encounter with the count and his warning words. "I think we need to talk in the morning. There's nothing we can do tonight. And we'll all think more clearly if we can get some sleep. Can you meet us here, at the pasticceria, in the morning?"

Valentina said, "What if he's already dead?"

"He's not," Emma said with more conviction than she felt. "They are waiting to see if you'll hand us over. We'll figure something out, Valentina. We'll get Marco back. Can you meet us here in the morning?"

When Valentina agreed, Emma urged her to try to rest, or even to sleep if possible, and then hung up to do the same herself.

The following morning, after getting almost no sleep at all, Emma woke Daniel early and told him about the ransom note.

As soon as the bakery opened, Emma, Daniel, and Valentina huddled at a corner table of Pasticceria Ricci, speaking in hushed tones, plates of nougat cake and cups of coffee on the table.

Daniel shook his head. "We can't just hand ourselves over. That's suicide."

"But we can't let them hurt Marco either," Valentina insisted.

Emma leaned in. "What if we get into that secret entrance tonight? We might find evidence we can take to the police tomorrow."

"It's risky," Daniel said, frowning. "I don't like the idea of going there in the dark."

"So is doing nothing," Emma countered. "We don't have much time."

Valentina nodded. "I'll take you there at low tide. That will be just after midnight. But what if we don't find anything?"

Emma squeezed her hand. "We have to try. It's our best shot at saving Marco without getting ourselves killed."

Daniel sighed. "I still don't like this." He took a bite of the nougat cake. "But I don't see another option. Promise me," he looked at both women in turn, "that you will not go rushing off or do anything stupid."

Emma sat back and stared at him. "Am I known for doing stupid things?"

Daniel gave a sheepish shake of his head. "No. But you scared me, Em. Going off without me the other night. I don't know what I'd do if I lost you."

She took his hands in hers. "Then you promise too. Because I don't want to lose you either."

Daniel nodded and smiled at her. "I promise."

"All right," Emma said. "Let's meet here at 11 PM. That should give us enough time to get to the church and check things out before the tide comes back in."

As Daniel headed upstairs to answer emails and Valentina returned to work, Emma tied on her apron, finally ready for a day of baking with Lucia. The familiar routine of measuring and mixing ingredients was sure to sooth her frayed nerves.

"And so, at last, we make meringues," Lucia said with a smile. "No trips to Murano today. Just baking. There are many flavors we can make. What do you choose?"

Emma scanned the array of ingredients on the counter. "How about lemon, raspberry, and chocolate?"

Lucia nodded approvingly. "Good choices. We'll start with lemon."

As they whipped egg whites and sugar, Emma's mind wandered to the night ahead. But Lucia's voice snapped her back to the present.

"Emma, you're over-beating. Soft peaks, remember?"

"Sorry," Emma said, slowing her mixer. "I guess I'm a little distracted."

Lucia studied her face. "Trouble with your young man?"

Emma sighed. "It's complicated."

They worked in companionable silence, piping delicate swirls onto baking sheets. As the first batch baked, filling the kitchen with a citrusy aroma, Lucia turned to Emma.

"Now, nougat cake. You make the cake today, and I will keep an eye on you while making pastries."

Emma gathered her ingredients, grateful for the chance to focus on the process. She poured honey into a heavy-bottomed pan and began to stir.

As she stirred, her thoughts drifted. Giuseppe's death, the danger Valentina and Marco were in, Daniel's silence about the job in St. Paul - it all swirled in her mind like the honey in the pan.

"Keep stirring," Lucia reminded her gently as she folded butter into dough for a flaky pastry. "Patience is key."

Emma nodded, focusing on the slow caramelization of the honey. The repetitive motion was oddly comforting.

"Lucia," Emma said after a while, "have you ever had to make a big decision about your future?"

Lucia chuckled. "Many times, *cara*. Life is full of big decisions."

"How do you know what's right?"

Lucia considered this. "Sometimes, you don't. You make the best choice you can with what you know."

Emma pondered this as she continued stirring. Finally, the honey reached the perfect amber color.

"Now, add the egg whites," Lucia instructed.

Emma carefully poured the hot honey into the whipped egg whites, watching as the mixture transformed into a glossy, pale gold.

"Beautiful," Lucia praised. "You have a natural touch."

As Emma folded in the nuts and fruit and shaped the cake, she felt a sense of accomplishment. Despite the chaos in her life, she could still create something perfect.

Chapter 20

Emma's heart raced as she, Daniel, and Valentina glided silently through the dark waters of Venice. The city was eerily quiet, save for the gentle lapping of water against stone.

Emma's eyes widened as Valentina steered the gondola closer to the ancient church wall. The water level had dropped, revealing a low stone archway that had been completely submerged earlier.

"I can't believe it," Emma whispered, her voice barely audible over the gentle lapping of water against stone. "There really is an entrance here."

Daniel leaned forward, his brow furrowed. "It's so well-hidden. No wonder we couldn't see it before, during high tide. The steps leading down to it were under water. The entire entrance was underwater."

Valentina nodded, her expression less surprised than her companions. "Venice has many secrets like this. Old passageways, forgotten tunnels. But I never knew about this one."

As they drew nearer, Emma could make out the faint outline of stone stairs beyond the entrance, leading upward into darkness. The air coming from the entrance was cool and damp, carrying a musty scent.

"Should we go in?" Emma asked, her hand hovering near the slimy stone edge.

Daniel hesitated. "It looks pretty dark in there. And narrow. We could take this location to the police and let them handle it."

"I don't know what's waiting for us at the top of those stairs," Valentina said, her voice low. "But I'm certain there are answers."

Emma ran her fingers along the rough stone, feeling centuries of history beneath her touch. The smell of stagnant water and mold filled her nostrils, making her wrinkle her nose.

With determination in her voice, Emma said, "We need to find out what's going on."

Daniel nodded, his face grim in the moonlight. "I actually agree. Let's hope this leads us somewhere useful."

As Valentina maneuvered the gondola closer, Emma caught sight of movement in the small square beside the church.

"Wait," she hissed, grabbing Daniel's arm. "Someone's coming."

They froze, hardly daring to breathe as a couple strolled by, arm in arm, their laughter echoing off the ancient stones.

Once the couple had passed, Valentina steered the gondola to the edge of the archway. "We have a problem," she said softly. "If we all go in, the gondola will be a dead giveaway that we're inside."

Emma bit her lip, considering. "You're right. Daniel and I will go in. Can you tie up somewhere nearby and come back?"

Valentina nodded. "Be careful. Please. I can't lose any more friends. I'll be back as soon as I can."

Daniel stepped out first, offering his hand to Emma. The stone was slick under her feet, and she gripped his hand tightly.

"Ready?" he asked.

Emma took a deep breath. "As I'll ever be."

They crouched down, peering into the inky blackness beyond the archway.

"Good luck," Valentina whispered. "I'll be right behind you."

As Valentina's gondola slipped away into the night, Emma and Daniel exchanged a look. Then, without a word, Daniel ducked under the archway and disappeared into the unknown.

Emma's heart pounded as she watched Valentina's gondola slip away into the darkness. She turned back to the low stone archway, ready to follow Daniel inside, when a familiar voice shattered the silence.

"Emma? What in the world are you doing down there?"

Emma froze, her blood turning to ice. She looked up to see Bob's bright flamingo shirt and his bewildered face peering down at them from the small square above.

"Bob?" she hissed, panic rising in her throat. "What are *you* doing here?"

Daniel's head popped back out of the archway. "Is that Bob? Again?"

Bob's voice echoed off the ancient stones. "I was just out for a midnight stroll. Venice is so beautiful at night, don't you think? But what are you two up to? Is there some kind of secret tunnel tour I didn't know about?"

Emma's mind raced. How could Bob be here, of all places, at this exact moment?

Daniel tugged on her pant leg and Emma bent to hear him whisper urgently, "This is too much of a coincidence. He's got to be involved somehow."

Emma sighed. Bob, of all people, seemed the least likely person to be part of Giuseppe's death and Marco's kidnapping.

But perhaps he could be useful. She called up to Bob, trying to keep her voice steady. "Bob, we are actually in a bit of trouble and need you to do something for us. Can you go get the police?"

Bob's eyebrows shot up. "The police?" His voice was so loud that surely he would wake anyone in the houses along the canal. "Oh, I don't know about that. I'm not really comfortable—"

"Bob," Daniel cut in, his voice sharp. "Get down here. Now."

Bob hesitated, then made his way down to the water's edge. As soon as he was close enough, Daniel grabbed him by the shirt and pulled him towards the archway.

"Hey! What's the big idea?" Bob protested loudly.

Daniel clamped a hand over Bob's mouth. "Are you part of this? The cash deliveries? Giuseppe's death?"

Bob's eyes widened in shock. He shook his head vigorously.

"Then why are you always showing up?" Emma demanded. "It can't be a coincidence."

Bob tried to speak, but his words were muffled by Daniel's hand. He was gesticulating wildly, his voice rising in volume despite Daniel's efforts to keep him quiet.

Daniel looked at Emma, his expression grim. "Oh my gosh. What an idiot."

Without waiting for a response, Daniel dragged a protesting Bob through the low stone entrance. Emma hesitated for a split second, then with one final glance around the deserted square, followed them into the darkness.

Chapter 21

E mma's heart raced as she followed Daniel and Bob into the dark passage. The beam from her phone's flashlight danced across damp stone walls, revealing a narrow staircase leading upward.

"Watch your step," she whispered, her voice echoing in the confined space. "Thank heavens I'm scared of heights and not claustrophobic," she whispered in an attempt to lighten the mood.

Bob stumbled, nearly falling backward onto Emma. Through Daniel's hand, which was still clamped over his mouth, he was trying to say something. Emma thought she might have caught the word 'ridiculous' as Daniel's hand loosened for a second, but it was hard to tell.

Daniel tightened his grip on Bob's arm. "Quiet," he hissed. "We don't know who might hear us."

They climbed the stairs, then descended another flight, the air growing colder and mustier with each step. Emma's light caught puddles scattered across the uneven floor.

"Look," she breathed, pointing ahead.

The passage opened into a vast chamber. Emma swept her light across the room, revealing tile mosaics of winged lions and eerie paintings of horses, men and skeletons adorning the walls. Her breath caught as the beam illuminated the row of skeletal figures staring back at them.

Daniel said quietly, "Will you be quiet if I let you go?"

Bob nodded furiously making the flamingos on his shirt bounce up and down.

"And will you try to run? If you do, I'll tackle you."

Bob shook his head and tried to say something.

Daniel took his hand off the other man's mouth.

"I won't run," Bob said after clearing his throat. "But what the hell do you think you're doing? And what is this place?"

Daniel releasing his hold on Bob but didn't step away. "It's some kind of crypt," he said.

Emma's feet splashed in shallow water as she examined the chamber. Cross vaults loomed overhead, supported by squat columns that disappeared into the gloom. Some of the columns were broken and crumbling. Some were in such pristine condition they could have been built last year.

Emma turned back to see Bob turning to Daniel, his jovial disposition replaced by indignation.

"And what the hell do you think you're doing?" Bob hissed. "Dragging me down here like some kind of kidnapper?"

Daniel's jaw clenched. "Keep your voice down," he warned.

"I will not," Bob shot back, though he did lower his volume slightly. "You owe me an explanation."

Emma tried to quiet Bob, holding up her hands. "We can't tell you anything, Bob. It's complicated."

Bob's eyes narrowed. "Complicated? I'll tell you what's complicated. You two, sneaking around in the middle of the night, dragging me into some kind of... underground crypt? This is insanity!"

Daniel's voice low. "How about you explain something to us, Bob? How is it that you keep showing up wherever we go? Are you following us?"

"Following you?" Bob sputtered as he stepped backward into a puddle. "That's ridiculous!"

"Is it?" Daniel pressed. "What do you know about the death of a gondolier named Giuseppe? Or about cash being smuggled through Venice?"

Bob's eyes widened. "Cash smuggling? A dead gondolier? What are you talking about?"

Emma studied Bob's face, searching for any sign of deception. His confusion seemed genuine, but she couldn't be sure.

"Come on," Daniel said, his tone skeptical. "You expect us to believe this is all just coincidence? How did you show up out there tonight? Do you expect us to believe you just happened to be on a midnight stroll in that tiny, out of the way church square?"

Bob threw up his hands. "I don't know what to tell you! Is this some kind of game? Are you filming a movie or something?"

Daniel scoffed. "A game? A man is dead, Bob. And you keep showing up at all the places connected to his death."

"Look," Bob said, his voice pleading, "I'm just a tourist. I don't know anything about any of this."

Emma glanced at Daniel. Was Bob a really good actor? Or was he truly as clueless as he seemed?

As Daniel and Bob continued arguing, Emma looked around the crypt. She noticed a small window high up on one wall, covered by a metal grate. No light filtered through – it was well past midnight.

Emma's eyes adjusted to the dim light as she moved deeper into the crypt. The flashlight on her phone cast eerie shadows across the ancient stone walls. She stepped carefully through the shallow water, her shoes making soft splashing sounds with each step.

The air was heavy with moisture and the musty scent of centuries-old stillness. Emma ran her hand along one of the short columns, feeling the cold, damp stone beneath her fingers. The cross vaults above seemed to press down on her, adding to the claustrophobic atmosphere.

She approached one of the stone sarcophagi and by the light of her phone, saw that its lid was carved with intricate designs barely visible in the low light. Emma wondered who might be entombed inside, and the thought made her shudder.

She lifted her phone to the paintings on the walls. Faded frescoes depicted scenes of winged lions and skeletal figures. Some areas had crumbled away, leaving gaps in the imagery like missing pieces of a macabre puzzle.

As Emma moved her phone's light further into the crypt, she suddenly stopped.

Several metal tables stood in the back at one side of the room. In stark contrast to the ancient surroundings, the tables held modern equipment. Printers, and what looked like cutting machines, as well as cardboard boxes, sat on the tables and on a stone sarcophagus, their sleek surfaces and modern office vibe out of place among the crumbling stone.

Just as she realized what she was seeing, her foot caught on something submerged in the water. She bent down and picked up a waterlogged bundle of papers. She unfolded them and her eyes widened. They were hundred-euro notes, damp and held together with a rubber band.

She took a few cautious steps toward the modern equipment. Her breath caught in her throat as she saw it in more detail.

"Daniel," she called, her voice barely above a whisper. "You need to see this."

Spread out atop several stone sarcophagi was an elaborate printing setup. Stacks of paper, ink bottles, and what looked like specialized printing equipment covered the ancient stone surfaces. Emma's gaze fell on one open coffin, stuffed to the brim with crisp euro bills.

Above the macabre counterfeiting operation, a glittering mosaic caught her eye. A man on horseback, spear raised, battled a fierce dragon. Emma wondered briefly who the man was. He looked ready to spear whoever was running the counterfeit printing presses.

"What is it?" Daniel's voice came from behind her. "Holy sh—"

Bob followed Daniel and stared, his mouth open, his flamingo shirt absurdly out of place in the ancient archway.

Emma shook her head, still processing the scene before her. She swept her phone's light over the room once more, and she froze as the light landed on a dark shape slumped against one of the stone columns.

"Marco?" she gasped, rushing forward.

The glass artist was chained to the column, his head lolling to one side. His dark hair was matted with something that might be blood. Emma dropped to her knees beside him, checking for signs of life.

"He's breathing," she gasped. "Oh, thank heavens."

Bob's face drained of color. "This... this isn't a game, is it?"

Chapter 22

E mma watched as Bob's eyes widened with panic. He stumbled backward, nearly tripping over his own feet.

"I'm outta here," Bob yelped, spinning around and bolting for the entrance.

Daniel lunged forward, grabbing Bob's arm. "Hold it right there."

Bob struggled against Daniel's grip. "Let me go! I don't want any part of this!"

"Listen to me," Daniel said, his voice low and urgent. "If you run now, your life could be in danger. These people are serious, and they would definitely think you're involved."

Bob's face went pale. "But I'm not! I swear!"

"That might be true," Emma said, stepping closer. "But they don't know that. Right now, the safest thing for you is to stick with us."

Bob's shoulders slumped. He stumbled over to the nearest sarcophagus and leaned heavily against it, sliding down until he was sitting on the damp floor.

"Oh Gosh," he moaned, burying his face in his hands. "What have I gotten myself into?"

Emma knelt beside him, placing a hand on his shoulder. "It's going to be okay, Bob. We'll figure this out together."

Bob looked up at her, his eyes wide with fear. "I just wanted to see Venice," he said, his voice trembling. "I never thought I'd end up in some... some underground crypt with counterfeit money and unconscious people."

Daniel looked down at Bob. "You sounded pretty pumped about being in a spy movie the other day on the Bridge of Sighs."

When Bob just gazed up at Daniel with a terrified expression, Daniel's gaze softened. "OK, listen. We need to work together to get out safely. We're doing our best."

Emma knelt beside Marco. He was slumped against the column, eyes closed, a gag covering his mouth. She tugged at the chains that were binding him to the column. "These aren't budging. We need to find a way to get him out of here." She scanned the equipment in the dimly lit crypt. "Do you think there's a key somewhere?"

"Even if there was, we don't have time to search," Daniel said. "I might be able to pick the lock, but I'd need tools and time."

Emma rummaged through her purse. "I've got tweezers. Would those work?"

Daniel took them and knelt to examine the lock. "Maybe, but it's a long shot."

As Daniel fiddled with the lock, Emma pulled out her phone. "I'll text Valentina, tell her to bring... I don't know... bolt cutters or something."

She tapped at her screen, frowning. "Seriously? No service down here."

Bob whimpered, wringing his hands.

Emma turned her phone to the equipment and started snapping photos of the counterfeit operation and then of Marco. "Evidence," she muttered.

Daniel stood up, shaking his head. "This isn't working. Although the tweezers were a good idea, Em." He put a hand on her arm, and she stopped snapping photos. "We need to get the police."

"But what about Marco?" she protested. "We can't just leave him! They're going to kill him when we don't show up tonight."

"We can't free him ourselves," Daniel said. "Our best bet is to get help fast. The longer we stay down here, the more likely we'll get caught."

Emma hesitated, looking at Marco's unconscious form. She shook her head. "I hate it. But I think you're right." She glanced at Bob and whispered, "What about him?"

Daniel sighed and whispered, "Do our best to keep him quiet, I suppose."

Emma nodded reluctantly, her gaze lingering on Marco's still form. "Okay, let's go."

As they turned to go, Emma froze. Voices were echoing along the stone passageways from the direction they'd come.

She and Daniel stared at each other.

Then Daniel grabbed her arm, pulling her behind the sarcophagus where Bob was slouched.

"What's going on?" Bob whispered.

Emma shook her head and put a finger to her lips, and Bob's eyes widened as they darted to the passage.

They crouched low, pressing themselves against the cold stone. Emma held her breath, straining to hear.

"Maybe it's Valentina," she breathed, barely audible.

The footsteps grew louder, accompanied by unfamiliar male voices. Emma's hope faded.

A sharp intake of breath made her turn. Bob's eyes were wide with panic, his mouth opening to cry out.

Daniel lunged, clamping a hand over Bob's mouth and dragging him back down beside them. Bob struggled, but Daniel held firm.

"Quiet," Daniel hissed in Bob's ear. "Or we're all dead."

Emma leaned against the sarcophagus, her heart racing. The voices were getting closer. Any second now, whoever it was would enter the crypt.

Chapter 23

E mma's heart pounded as she crouched behind the sarcophagus, her shoulder pressed against Bob's. She could feel Bob trembling, Daniel's hand still firmly over his mouth.

Footsteps echoed through the crypt, growing louder. Emma held her breath as she leaned slightly forward to see two figures emerge from the shadows.

Her eyes widened in disbelief. It was Count Casanova, accompanied by a man who looked familiar but who she didn't immediately recognize.

"*È tutto pronto per stasera?*" the count asked in a low voice.

The other man nodded. "*Sì, Conte. I pacchetti sono pronti.*"

Emma's Italian was limited, but she caught enough to understand they were discussing something about tonight. She glanced at Daniel, seeing her own shock mirrored in his eyes. Daniel mouthed the word, 'count,' and Emma nodded.

Emma pulled back out of sight as she heard the count striding over to where Marco sat unconscious. He asked something in Italian.

"Still out cold," his companion replied, switching to English. "What about the American tourists?"

"If Valentina doesn't deliver them tonight, we'll need to take care of it ourselves," the count said coldly. "They've seen too much. I don't know how that woman managed to get American detectives involved, but I hardly believe it was an accident. Women butting in where they don't belong. She should never have been allowed to be a gondolier in the first place. Those friends of hers have to be Interpol, or at the very least, FBI. We can't risk them finding evidence. I will dispose of them myself if I have to."

Emma's blood ran cold. She felt Daniel tense beside her.

"And the money?" the other man asked.

The count gave a small snort. "By this time tomorrow, a hundred million in counterfeit euros will be safely out of Italy. Our buyers are eager."

Emma felt her foot slip on the damp stone floor. She tried not to breathe.

"Should we move him?" the count's companion asked.

"No need. Once we've dealt with the Americans, we'll get rid of him too. Unlike Giuseppe, this one won't need to deliver a warning with his corpse. We can dispose of him in the sea."

Emma thought she might faint from trying so hard not to breathe.

Beside her, Bob was trembling. He opened his mouth and blinked quickly several times.

And then, he sneezed.

Daniel reacted in a heartbeat. His jumped to his feet and with a surge of strength, he shoved the heavy stone lid of the sarcophagus. It teetered for a split second before crashing to the floor with a deafening boom that echoed through the crypt.

Emma jumped up.

As the count and his companion whirled toward the noise, she darted forward, swinging her purse at the nearest man with all her might. It connected with the back of the man's head with a solid thwack.

As the man stumbled, Emma realized it was the servant she'd seen at the count's house- Roberto. A half second later, she caught sight of something metallic glinting in his waistband. A gun.

Time seemed to slow as Roberto fumbled for the weapon. Emma lunged forward, her fingers closing around the cold metal just as he pulled it free.

"Let go!" he snarled, trying to wrench the gun from her grasp.

Emma gritted her teeth, a growl like an animal coming from her throat, her knuckles white as she clung to the weapon.

Roberto tried to lift the gun toward Emma, but she raised her knee in a swift kick at his crotch, and his grip slackened as he yelled in pain.

With a sharp twist, she pried the gun from his grip. The weight of it felt foreign and terrifying in her hand.

Roberto was doubled over, staring at her in fear and pain.

Across the crypt, Daniel tackled the count. They hit the stone floor hard, grappling and rolling across the damp stones.

"You fool," the count spat, his elegant facade dissolving as he fought. "You have no idea who you're dealing with!"

Daniel grunted in response as he struggled to pin the older man down. "I know enough," he panted.

A crash from behind made Emma spin around.

Bob, eyes wide with terror, had stumbled backward into the printing press. The massive machine wobbled dangerously, metal parts clanking.

As Emma was distracted, Roberto stumbled forward. With a roar of rage, he charged at her.

Emma lifted the gun at him, terrified when he didn't stop charging toward her.

At the last second, as she was trying to tell herself to pull the trigger and he was about to tackle her, Emma sidestepped.

Roberto, unable to stop, slammed into the already unsteady printing press.

"No!" the count grunted from where he struggled with Daniel.

But it was too late. With an ear-splitting screech, the printing press toppled. It crashed into one of the ancient pillars near the entrance, the one that had been leaning precariously.

For a moment, everything seemed to freeze.

Then, with a thunderous crack, the pillar shattered.

Emma watched, dumbfounded, as chunks of stone and centuries-old mortar cascaded down filling the entrance to the crypt with debris. Dust billowed up, filling rooms with choking filth. She coughed and waved her free hand, trying to clear the air.

Bob whimpered from where he cowered against the wall.

Another crash made Emma spin around.

Daniel, wrestling with the count, had toppled a stack of wooden crates full or euros. Bills were flying up to the arched ceiling and fluttering down all around them. The count slipped on a stack of bills and landed hard on the stone floor.

There was a groan and Emma whirled around gripping the gun in her shaking hands. Roberto, half-buried under the debris he'd caused to crash down, groaned again. She pointed the gun at him and shouted, "Stay where you are!"

But his eyes were closed, and after another small moan, he lay motionless beneath the crumbled stones. A stone had hit his head, she realized, and he was as unconscious as Marco.

A few euros fluttered past her and landed beside Bob. As Daniel and the count struggled behind her, Emma turned, looking through the dust at where the entrance had been. It was completely blocked by the collapsed archway.

The count let out a roar of anger as he leapt back to his feet and tackled Daniel.

But Emma hardly noticed as she realized they were trapped.

Chapter 24

E mma's heart raced as she surveyed the chaos around her, searching for a way out.

Bob, his face pale and sweating, was frantically scooping up handfuls of counterfeit bills and stuffing them into his pockets.

"What are you doing?"

He looked at her, wild-eyed. "Well, I-I don't know! I mean, all this money!"

Emma shook her head in disbelief and rushed to Marco. A few smaller rocks had landed on his legs, and he was stirring slightly, a low groan escaping his lips.

She knelt at his side, careful to keep the gun pointed away from him. "Marco? Can you hear me?" She patted his cheek, then shook his shoulder.

His eyelids fluttered, then slowly opened. "What... where am I?" he mumbled, his voice hoarse.

"You're in an underground crypt," Emma said. "Count Casanova kidnapped you. We came to rescue you, but-"

"Valentina?" Marco interrupted, his eyes suddenly wide with panic. "Where's Valentina?"

Emma's stomach dropped. Valentina. In all the chaos, she'd forgotten the gondolier was supposed to return. "She... she was supposed to join us. But she never came in."

Marco struggled weakly against his chains. "We have to find her! What if they got her too?" His voice was horse, his words slurred.

"You need to stay still," Emma said as her mind raced. Marco was right. Where was she? "Valentina was going to tie up her gondola and come back, but..."

A crash from behind made Emma whirl around. Daniel had pinned the count against a sarcophagus, but the older man was putting up a fierce fight.

"Emma!" Daniel called out, his voice strained. "A little help here!"

"Oh, yes!" With a quick glance back at Marco, she ran toward Daniel, gun pointing at the count.

But as she rushed forward, Bob, frantically grabbing at a pile of euros near Daniel, slipped in a patch of inky water. His feet went out from under him. He flailed wildly.

"Look out!" she cried, but it was too late.

Bob slipped right into the fight. His legs collided with the count's ankle. The count toppled backward with a startled yelp as Daniel released him.

Leaping over Bob, who was sprawled in the inky puddle, Daniel tackled the older man to the ground, knocking another table of printing equipment to the stone floor.

"Got you!" Daniel grunted, pinning the count face-down and wrenching the gun from his grasp.

Bob got to his hands and knees beside Daniel, still shoving euros into his shirt pocket.

"Bob!" Daniel shouted. "Take off your shirt and give it to Emma!"

Bob turned to Daniel with wide eyes. "What? Why?"

"Just do it!" Daniel shouted, struggling to keep the count subdued.

"But... but the money is everywhere, and this is my favorite shirt," Bob said, sitting back and clutching at the garish flamingo-patterned pocket bulging with counterfeit bills.

Emma rushed to him and started unbuttoning his shirt. "For heaven's sake, Bob! This is no time to worry about fashion!"

Reluctantly, Bob peeled off his shirt, euros falling from where he had stuffed them, and handed it to Emma who looked at Daniel for instructions.

"I need strips to tie him with," Daniel said as his knee dug into the count's back.

Emma used her teeth to make small tears in the flamingo fabric and then tore the shirt into strips. She handed them to Daniel.

In one swift motion, Daniel used the pink and green fabric to bind the count's hands and feet.

As Emma watched him work, a faint trickling sound caught her attention. She looked around, and as she glanced toward the blocked entrance, she blinked in confusion at what she saw.

Water was seeping through the crumbled stoned and debris, dribbling over the rocks and forming growing puddles on the stone floor.

"Oh mt gosh. The tide is rising," Emma whispered.

She watched as Daniel stood over the count who squirmed against his makeshift bonds. The count's gun was gripped in Daniel's hand.

"Don't even think about it," Daniel warned, his voice low and steady.

The count tried to glare up at him but caught sight of his own gun and stopped struggling.

Emma looked back at the incoming water. "It can't get too deep in here, right?" She walked to the count and glared at him. "How high does the water get in here?"

Count Casanova glanced at Daniel and the gun, then said in a bitter voice, "The water never came in here more than a centimeter or so. But your bumbling seems to have created a new opening to the canal." He looked toward the water seeping in more quickly. "I have never seen it like this. Please," he said to Daniel. "Untie me or I will drown. You don't want to be a murderer, do you?"

Daniel rolled his eyes. "He's lying. The floor was damp. Water must come in all the time."

But Emma, seeing how quickly the water was coming in, wasn't so sure. "It's already higher than the water marks on the wall," she said.

"Your woman is correct," the count said, rising panic evident in his voice. "This is not normal! That column has collapsed. There is a breach in the wall and the tide waters are coming in. We are on a lower level. You don't know Venice like I do. We will drown!"

"Be quiet," Daniel commanded. "Let me see what we can find."

Looking desperately around for another way out, Emma saw again the high window she'd noticed earlier.

"Bob," she said, turning to the now-shirtless tourist. "I need your help."

Bob's eyes were wide with panic. "More than my shirt? All these euros are useless if we can't get out! We're trapped! We're going to drown!"

"No, we're not," Emma said firmly. She pointed to the window. "Do you see that? I might be able to open it. Come on."

She grabbed Bob's arm and pulled him toward the pile of fallen debris beneath the window.

Bob hesitated.

"It's our only shot," Emma insisted. "Now climb."

Reluctantly, Bob followed her lead. They made their way carefully up the uneven mound of stone and mortar, sending small cascades of rubble sliding down with each step.

At the top, Emma turned to Bob. "I need you to boost me up."

Bob's face paled. "But-"

"No buts. Cup your hands like this." She demonstrated. "I'll use them as a step."

Bob nodded, his hands shaking as he formed a foothold. "But I might slip."

Ignoring his comment, Emma took a deep breath and placed her foot in his palms.

"Ready?" she asked.

"No," Bob replied.

"Too bad. On three. One... two... three!"

Bob heaved upward as Emma pushed off. She grabbed the narrow ledge beneath the window, her fingers scrabbling for purchase on the damp stone. For a heart-stopping moment, she thought she might fall. Her vision wavered with the familiar vertigo. Then her grip firmed, her vision cleared, and she pulled herself up.

The ledge was barely wide enough for her to perch on. Emma pressed her back against the wall, trying not to look down.

"You okay up there?" Daniel called from below, the gun still trained on the count.

Emma's stomach churned as she glanced down at the crypt floor, now several feet below her. She swallowed hard.

"Yep. I have to be," she replied, her voice only slightly higher than its normal pitch.

She clung to the narrow ledge, her fingers aching as she worked at the rusted window latch. Below, water now sloshed around Daniel's ankles as stood beside the bound and terrified count.

"Please," the count begged, his voice rising with panic. "The water's coming in too fast. I'm telling you the truth. The water has never come in like this before. Do you think I would run my business in a place that flooded regularly? You must let me go!"

Daniel's jaw clenched. "Not a chance."

"But we'll all drown!"

"Shut up," Daniel snapped.

In a trembling voice, Bob asked, "Any luck with that window?"

Emma's fingers slipped on the corroded metal. "It's stuck tight. I can't budge it."

The water level crept higher, now lapping at the unconscious Roberto's face. Daniel, keeping the gun on the count, moved slowly across the crypt and dragged Roberto to higher ground.

"Bob," Emma said, "I need to come down. This isn't working. Maybe I can find a rock or something to hit it with."

She looked down at Bob, who stood unsteadily atop the rubble pile. His face was pale, his eyes wide with fear.

"I-I don't know if I can catch you," he stammered.

"Just help me down slowly," Emma said. "I'll-"

But as Bob looked up, his foot slipped. He windmilled his arms, trying to regain balance. The pile of debris shifted beneath him.

With a yelp, he tumbled backward landing on his backside. The mound of rubble collapsed, sliding away in a miniature avalanche. When the dust settled, Bob was sitting in knee-deep water, and Emma was stranded on the ledge, with no way down.

"Emma!" Daniel called, dropping the gun to his side and stepping away from the count.

"Stop!" Emma shouted as the count tried to wriggle to his hands and feet.

Daniel whirled back around and trained the gun back on the only member of Italian royalty they had ever met.

Emma pressed her back against the wall, heart pounding. Vertigo was making the crypt spin. "I can't get down," she whispered.

Chapter 25

E mma clung to the ledge, her fingers aching from the strain, her head swimming with fear. She closed her eyes and took a deep breath, remembering Daniel's words on the tower.

"I have solid ground under me," she whispered, focusing on the feel of stone beneath her knees and hands. "I am safe. I am on solid stone ground."

"Emma?" Daniel said.

She nodded. "I'm on solid ground," she whispered a little louder. She managed to open her eyes and look at him.

"Do you trust me?" Daniel asked, his eyes locked on hers.

Her stomach lurched, not only at the vertigo, but at his question. She thought suddenly of the blue and green vase, and the job offer in St. Paul. She thought of the first time they worked together on a murder case back in Whispering Pines. Her mind flashed to all the times she had been in danger, and Daniel had protected her. With a jolt, she realized the vase and the job offer didn't matter. She did trust him. Despite the questions about the job and uncertainty about the future, she knew Daniel would do everything in his power to protect and take care of her.

"I do," she whispered, knowing it was true. "I trust you."

Daniel nodded and raised the gun.

Despite herself, Emma sucked in a breath.

"Scoot back as far as you can into the corner and cover your head with your arms."

"Oh golly," Bob said in a barely audible voice. "Hey man, it's going to be ok. You don't have to shoot her!"

Emma pressed herself against the wall, her arms shielding her face. She squeezed her eyes shut.

"Hey, stop!" Bob shouted.

Three sharp cracks echoed through the crypt. Glass tinkled down and a shard of ancient wood flew past Emma as she tried to cover her ears more tightly. Then she felt a rush of cool night air.

"It's clear!" Daniel shouted. "The lock is gone. Push the window open!"

Emma lowered her arms and saw the shattered remains of the window frame. She shoved at the loosened pane, and it swung outward with a rusty groan.

"Go get help! And hurry!" Daniel yelled as Emma gripped the window's edge.

She paused, looking down at Daniel and the others still trapped in the rising water. "I can't leave you here!"

"Yes, you can!" Daniel insisted. "There's no way for us to reach you. And you're the only one who fits through. Go get help!"

Emma's chest tightened. She knew he was right, but the thought of abandoning them made her stomach churn. "I'll be back as fast as I can," she promised.

With one last look at Daniel, Emma squeezed through the jagged opening, glass shards scraping her arms. She tumbled onto a narrow stone ledge, the cool night air a surprising contrast to the damp crypt. The smell of the canal hit her nostrils.

A garbage boat chugged along the dark water, its engine sputtering. Without waiting to think, Emma leaped.

She landed with a thud on the deck and rolled to her side, startling the worker who let out an exclamation in Italian.

"*Polizia*!" Emma shouted, her voice cracking as she struggled to her feet. "Please, take me to the police!"

The boatman's eyes widened, but he nodded, quickening the boat's speed.

As they sped through the canals, Emma's hands shook as she pulled out her phone. Signal bars appeared, and she dialed emergency services.

"There's a flooding crypt," she gasped. "People trapped. Counterfeiters. My friends—"

The voice on the other end said something in Italian that Emma didn't understand. Then the voice said, "Wait. I get English."

After a few seconds that felt like eternity, a new voice came on the line. "Can I help you?"

Emma rattled off directions again. "There's a flooding crypt," she said, explaining about the entrance and the people trapped and giving the location the best she could.

"Ok," the man on the other end said. "We are sending someone now." He hung up.

Having done all she could about that now, Emma's thoughts turned to Valentina. Where was she? Her fingers flew across the screen again, dialing Valentina's number.

"Come on, pick up," she muttered. The phone rang once, twice, three times, then went to voicemail.

"Valentina, it's Emma! Where are you? Are you okay? Call me back!"

There was a beep at the end of the voicemail, and Emma lowered the phone and stared at it. The rapid lapping of water against the boat's hull seemed to mimic her growing unease.

"Your friend is ok?" the boatman asked, his voice gruff but kind.

Emma shook her head "She was supposed to meet us. I don't know what happened."

The boat rounded a corner, and Emma caught sight of the police station's lights. She gripped the side of the boat, willing it to move faster.

"Almost there," the boatman said.

Emma's mind raced. Had Valentina been caught? Was she dead too?

The boat bumped against the dock, and Emma scrambled out.

"Thank you," she called over her shoulder, already running towards the station's entrance.

Emma burst through the police station doors, her heart pounding.

The room was surprisingly calm. One officer- a woman with her hair in a tidy bun- sat behind the front desk typing on a computer. Another officer, a man with grey hair and glasses, was shuffling papers.

"*Scusi*," she said breathlessly to the woman at the front desk. "I need to see—"

The officer said something in Italian and held up her finger as her phone rang.

"No, you don't understand!" Emma tried to push her way forward, but the officer held out her hand as she spoke into the phone.

Emma paused as she heard a snippet of the conversation. "...contraffatta... gondola..."

"Oh," Emma interrupted. "Do you mean *counterfeit*? And a gondola? Valentina Rossi? If you know where she is, please tell me!"

The officer frowned held the phone away from her ear and scowled at Emma. "What is this? What are you talking about?"

"Do you know where Valentina is?" Emma asked.

An older man in a crisp uniform stepped through a doorway and approached. "Her English is not so good," he said. "I am the senior officer here. What is the problem?"

Emma turned to him. "I think my friend, Valentina, might be in trouble! She was supposed to meet us at the crypt, the one that's flooding. And my boyfriend and some others are trapped there. The tide is coming in. I called in and reported it. Please, I need to know where Valentina is, if she's safe, and if someone is going to help them!"

The man scowled, studying Emma. "You are the American woman who called about the flooding crypt?"

Emma nodded. "Yes!"

"We have officers on the way now.

"Oh thank heavens." Emma let out a shaky breath. "The water is rising so fast! I came as quickly as I could."

"But what is this about the gondolier? Valentina Rossi?" the officer asked, his eyes narrowing.

"I need to know if she's safe! I think they might have killed her, like Giuseppe!"

The man held up his hand. "Slow down. What do you know about Giuseppe. You mean the gondolier who died?"

Emma took a deep breath and explained everything—the notebook, the coded messages, the packages Valentina was forced to deliver, counterfeiting operation, the count, and the flooding crypt. "But

I don't know why she didn't come back!" Emma finished, her eyes brimming with tears. "And all this time we've been talking, she could be in terrible danger!"

The officer regarded her for a moment in silence, and Emma thought he must be able to hear her heart hammering in her chest.

"Follow me," he said.

He led Emma down a narrow hallway to a row of holding cells.

"Oh gosh," Emma said. "Please don't arrest me. I swear I'm telling the truth. I have evidence on my phone. I forgot to show you the photos!"

The officer motioned to the last holding cell and Emma was about to tell him she was an American citizen and wanted a lawyer, when she saw what he was pointing to.

Huddled on a bench in the corner was-

Valentina!

Emma nearly crumpled with relief. "Valentina!"

Valentina's head snapped up. "Emma? Oh, thank heavens." She rushed to the bars. "I tried to come back, but these men—they forced me to take packages. They said they'd hurt Marco if I didn't. And then when I took them, they called the police and told them I was smuggling drug money!"

Emma gripped the bars. "I'm so glad you're alive! We found Marco. The police are rescuing them now."

Valentina held Emma's hands through the bars. "I tried to tell them what was happening, but they arrested me. They thought I was the one behind it all."

The senior officer cleared his throat. "*Scusi, signorina*. You mentioned evidence on your phone?"

About an hour later, Emma's heart leapt as Daniel, Marco, and Bob walked into the police station, followed by officers leading the handcuffed Count Casanova and his assistant, Roberto. Emma rushed to Daniel, throwing her arms around him.

"You're okay!" she exclaimed, burying her face in his chest.

Daniel hugged her tightly. "Thank you."

Emma pulled back, a wry smile on her face. "Thank *you* for not shooting me."

"Thank *you* for trusting me," Daniel replied, his eyes twinkling. "And for rescuing me."

Bob bounced on his heels, grinning from ear to ear. "This was amazing! A real-life spy movie!" He turned to the senior officer. "Say, will these criminals walk across the Bridge of Sighs?" He motioned to the count and Roberto. "And if so, can I film it on my cell phone? No one back at the office will believe this!"

The officer shook his head. "No, that's not how—"

"That's ok!" Bob interrupted. "I didn't think so. But could we at least take them there for a selfie?"

"Absolutely not," the officer said firmly.

Marco broke away from the group and asked, "Where is Valentina?"

"She's still in holding," the senior officer said, "as we verify everything Miss Harper has reported. But," he looked over the statements Emma and Valentina had given as well as the photos he'd printed off from Emma's phone, "I think we have enough." He picked up a large ring of keys and nodded toward the hallway. "Come."

Emma, Marco and the others followed him down the hall to where Valentina was waiting, perched on the bench, her eyes brimming with tears.

Marco rushed to Valentina's cell. "You're here! I was so worried."

Valentina reached through the bars, cupping Marco's face. "I am so sorry. Are you all right?"

"Yes, yes, I'm fine. And I'm sorry," Marco said. "Thank you for not listening to me. For bringing them to rescue me."

As the officer unlocked the holding cell, Valentina reached through the bars and bopped Marco on the nose. "You silly man. Did you really think I was the kind of girl who does what she's told?"

Marco laughed, his eyes soft. "That's what I love about you."

The cell door swung open, and Valentina rushed into Marco's arms.

Emma smiled at Daniel, and he whispered, "You've done it again. Another happy ending."

Chapter 26

Emma carefully piped the last of the meringue mixture onto the baking sheet, her tongue poking out in concentration. Then she stepped back, admiring the perfect, glossy peaks.

"Lucia, look! I think I've finally got it," she called out.

Lucia bustled over, wiping her flour-covered hands on her apron. She peered at Emma's handiwork, a smile spreading across her face. "*Brava*, Emma! Those are *bellissimo*."

Emma beamed with pride. "I can't believe how much I've learned in just a few lessons."

"You can already make macarons," Lucia said. "So meringues are not so difficult. Now, let's finish that nougat cake, shall we?" She gestured to the kitchen counter.

As they moved to the workstation where a golden disc of nougat waited, Emma grabbed the bowl of fresh berries she'd picked up at the market that morning.

"These raspberries are perfect," Emma said, carefully arranging them on top of the cake.

The bell above the pasticceria's door chimed and a boisterous group of tourists spilled in, their chatter filling the small shop.

"*Buongiorno!*" Lucia called out, wiping her hands and heading to the front.

Emma peeked around the corner, watching as Lucia greeted the newcomers. An elderly Italian man in a crisp linen shirt leaned on his cane, eyeing the display case.

"Ah, Signor Moretti! The usual?" Lucia asked.

The old man nodded, his eyes crinkling. "*Sì, sì*. And perhaps one of those lovely meringues as well?"

Emma's heart swelled with pride. She turned back to the nougat cake, adding a final flourish of sliced peaches around the edge.

Lucia returned, chuckling to Emma. "That Moretti, he comes in every day at the same time. You could set your watch by him."

"I love how your bakery feels like the heart of the neighborhood," Emma said.

"And I think yours is, too, back in Minnesota, yes?" Lucia smiled. "Now, let's get that nougat cake out front. I'm sure it won't last long."

They carried the finished cake to the display case, sliding it carefully onto a silver platter. Emma stood back, admiring her handiwork amid the bustle of the shop, her mind drifting to her own bakery in Whispering Pines.

She balanced the plate of meringues carefully as she climbed the narrow stairs to Daniel's room and knocked softly on his door.

"Come in," Daniel called.

Emma found him hunched over his laptop, brow furrowed in concentration. "I brought you a treat," she said, setting the plate down beside him.

Daniel's face lit up. "Thanks, Em. These look amazing."

She perched on the edge of his bed, fidgeting with the hem of her shirt. "So... any interesting emails?"

Daniel closed his laptop and turned to face her. "Actually, yeah. It's about that job in St. Paul."

Emma's heart dropped into her stomach. "Oh?"

Daniel took a deep breath. "I've been thinking about it a lot, and now that we have a minute to talk- you know, without chasing murderers- there's something I need to tell you."

Emma felt her stomach flop over. She looked down at the worn wood floor, suddenly finding herself unable to meet his eyes.

He reached for her chin and tipped her head up, his eyes finding hers.

Emma wanted to look away. She didn't want to hear it- didn't want to know that he was leaving her.

"The reason I've been considering this job is... well, because it would pay better," he said in a quiet voice.

She swallowed. She already knew that. But that wasn't a good reason for him to leave her.

"It would pay enough," he looked into her eyes, "that we could get married. I would be able to provide a nice house for you, like you deserve."

Emma's eyes widened. "What? Wait." She blinked, trying to let his words sink in. "I thought you wanted a bigger office. A promotion."

He shook his head.

"But what about that vase you bought? The one to go in your office? It won't even fit-"

He cut her off, a small smile on his lips. "I thought it would be nice to have in our house. If we were ever, you know, together." When Emma just stared at him, he said, "That's why I asked you to help me pick it out. So we'd have something to go in our home that we picked out here. Together. But Em, I don't want to marry you if I can't provide for you."

Emma stared. "We already have two nice houses in Whispering Pines."

He rubbed the back of his neck. "I know, but I thought maybe you'd want something more. You know," he shrugged, "if we ever started a family."

Emma felt a smile that she couldn't repress forming on her lips. "Oh, Daniel. I love my bakery. I love Whispering Pines. And I love you! If... if you were to propose someday, I'd want to stay right there, with the people we love."

Daniel's shoulders relaxed. "Really? You wouldn't want to move to a bigger place in the city?"

"Not at all," Emma said putting her arms around his neck. "Whispering Pines is home."

Daniel pulled her into a tight embrace. "I'm so relieved. I thought I needed to do this to give you the life you deserved."

Emma leaned back, meeting his eyes. "Venice is wonderful. Paris was amazing. But the life I want is with you, in our town. That's all I need."

Chapter 27

E mma settled into the gondola, carefully placing her basket of meringues between her feet. The evening air was cool and fragrant with the scent of jasmine wafting from nearby balconies.

Valentina stood at the stern, expertly guiding them through the narrow canals.

"This is perfect," Emma sighed, leaning against Daniel's chest.

Marco grinned from his seat across from them. "I have something for you, Emma." He reached into a small bag and pulled out a delicate glass sculpture. "To commemorate our adventure and our new friendship."

Emma gasped as he handed it to her. The sculpture depicted four figures in a gondola, their features captured in surprising detail. "Oh my goodness! It's beautiful, Marco. Thank you!"

"Valentina helped with the design," Marco said, squeezing his girlfriend's hand.

As they rounded a corner, the sound of an accordion drifted across the water. Emma closed her eyes, savoring the moment.

"Look!" Daniel suddenly exclaimed, pointing to a nearby bridge. "Is that who I think it is?"

Emma followed his gaze and burst out laughing. There, in all his tourist glory, including a garish flower-covered shirt, stood Bob. He was talking animatedly to a woman wearing a 1950s style dress covered in Italian flags and a stylish hat that wouldn't have been out of place at a British fashion show- except for the cluster of Italian flags protruding from the band.

"I can't believe it," Emma giggled. "They're perfect for each other!"

As they drifted closer, Bob's voice carried across the water. "...and that's how I helped take down an international counterfeiting ring!"

The woman gasped, clearly impressed. "Oh, Bob! You're so brave!" She laid one hand on Bob's massive belly and smiled up at him.

Daniel snorted. "Should we tell her the truth?"

Emma shook her head, still grinning. "Let him have his moment. Besides, who'd believe the real story?"

As they passed under the bridge, Bob spotted them. "Hey! It's my crime-fighting buddies!" He waved enthusiastically. "Emma! Daniel! Come meet Gladys!"

Valentina steered the gondola closer to the bank.

Emma waved back at Bob. "Having a good evening?" she called out.

"The best!" Bob beamed. "Gladys and I are going to get gelato. Want to join us?"

Emma glanced at Daniel, then at Marco and Valentina. They all shook their heads, trying to suppress their laughter.

"Thanks, Bob, but we're good," Emma replied. "You two have fun!"

As they glided away, the sound of Bob regaling Gladys with his heroic tales faded into the background, replaced once more by the gentle lapping of water against stone and the distant strains of a violin.

Hours later, Emma leaned against the stone railing of the small bridge as she waited for Daniel, her eyes tracing the shimmering patterns on the Grand Canal. The setting sun painted the water in hues of gold and pink, while a gentle breeze carried the scent of salt and distant flowers.

She smiled to herself, thinking of Daniel's mysterious hints about their next destination. What secret place could he be planning? Emma's mind raced with possibilities.

Daniel's footsteps approached, and he joined her at the railing holding two gelatos- raspberry for Emma and chocolate for himself. "Penny for your thoughts?"

Emma turned to him, eyes sparkling, as she dipped her spoon into the gelato. "I was just wondering about this secret location you mentioned. Where are you whisking me off to next, Detective Lindberg?"

Daniel grinned, a mischievous glint in his eye. "Well, Ms. Harper, how does Morocco sound?"

Emma's jaw dropped and she almost dropped her gelato. "Morocco? Are you serious?"

"As I've ever been," Daniel chuckled. "I thought we could explore the markets of Marrakech, maybe ride camels in the Sahara..."

"Oh my gosh," Emma breathed, her mind reeling with excitement. "Daniel, that's... that's amazing!"

He wrapped an arm around her, pulling her close. "After everything we've been through here, I figured we deserved another adventure. Hopefully, one with fewer counterfeiters and flooding crypts."

Emma laughed, resting her head on his shoulder. "I don't know, solving mysteries with you is kind of fun."

"Even when it involves nearly drowning?"

"Especially then," Emma teased. She paused, watching a gondola glide beneath the bridge. "But maybe we can stick to solving the mystery of where to find the best tagine and mint tea in Marrakech. I hear Moroccan food is amazing."

Daniel pressed a kiss to her temple. "Deal."

They stood in comfortable silence, savoring their gelato and watching the last rays of sunlight dance across the water. A seagull cried in the distance, and the breeze ruffled Emma's hair.

"You know," Emma said softly, "Planning this trip back in Whispering Pines, with the money from the jewels and those notes left in my travel guide, hoping Bridget and Jake would be ok managing the bakery for the summer, I never imagined our romantic getaway would turn out quite like this."

Daniel chuckled. "What, you didn't plan on uncovering an international counterfeiting ring?"

"Shockingly, no," Emma grinned. "But why not? When we're together, anything is possible."

She kissed him, long and slow.

When she stepped back, he whispered, "You taste so sweet. Would you do this all again, if you had the chance?"

"I wouldn't change a thing."

Visit Penelope Online

Visit Penelope online to get all her books, including FREE
books, discounts and her latest news!

www.PenelopeLoveletter.com

much love,
Penelope

Made in the USA
Middletown, DE
17 November 2024

64750550R00135